KATHLEEN

A YANKEE GIRL
AT GETTYSBURG

KATHLEEN
A YANKEE GIRL
AT GETTYSBURG

Formerly titled *A Yankee Girl at Gettysburg*

ALICE TURNER CURTIS

Illustrated

GRAMERCY BOOKS
New York • Avenel

This edition is published by Random House Value Publishing, Inc.,
40 Engelhard Avenue, Avenel, New Jersey 07001.

Printed and bound in the United States of America

Library of Congress Cataloging-in-Publication Data

Curtis, Alice Turner.
 Kathleen : a Yankee girl at Gettysburg / Alice Turner Curtis.
  p. cm.
 Summary: Follows the experiences of a spirited, courageous
eleven-year-old girl in the days surrounding the eventful Civil War
battle at Gettysburg.
 ISBN 0-517-14773-4
 1. Gettysburg (Pa.), Battle of, 1863—Juvenile fiction.
[1. Gettysburg (Pa.), Battle of, 1863—Fiction. 2. United
States—History—Civil War, 1861–1865—Campaigns—Fiction.]
I. Garner, Charles, ill. II. Title.
PZ7.C941Kat 1995
[Fic]—dc20   95–10995
                   CIP
                   AC

8 7 6 5 4 3 2 1

CONTENTS

SHE QUICKLY SLIPPED THE PACKAGE INTO HER POCKET.

Page 7

FOREWORD

"Two brothers on their way.
One wore blue and one wore gray."

The words of this old folk song were written at the time of the Civil War, the most chronicled, debated, and studied war that ever took place in our land. It not only pitted state against state but set family against family, brother against brother—each of them bitterly putting aside familial love to fight for what they believed.

The culmination of all this passion and anger can be found in Gettysburg, the site of one of the most significant battles of the Civil War. There, on a sprawling green meadow in Pennsylvania, about 93,000 Union soldiers fought against more than 70,000 Confederates—with total casualties of dead, wounded, or missing soldiers soaring past 50,000. Later, Abraham Lincoln would declare Gettysburg a national cemetery and would consecrate the ground with his famous

Gettysburg Address. He had no idea that his words would become so famous—or that Gettysburg would be visited by thousands of people throughout the years.

Nor did the young, spirited Kathleen Webb. She was in the crowd when Lincoln spoke at Gettysburg. She stood next to her parents in a new dress and, as did so many others, she wept for the great losses felt by both sides. Kathleen was there, as well, during the crucial days before, during, and after the Battle of Gettysburg. She had listened to the adults discussing the encroaching Confederacy while they sipped tea or hooked rugs. She had met the Southern general Robert E. Lee, and watched her idealistic fifteen-year-old brother Ted go off to join the Union Army, not knowing if she would ever see him again.

All this was part of Kathleen's story—which, thanks to author Alice Turner Curtis, we are able to enjoy today. As rich as the gold coins Kathleen plans to give to her friends, as exciting as the chase after her runaway horse, as authentic as her pink gingham dress, *Kathleen*: *A Yankee Girl at Gettysburg* captures a time and place long gone. Although a work of fiction, this entertaining tale of a young girl in Civil War times breathes life into the world of a century ago. Here are sprawling Pennsylvania farms, unmarred by telephone poles or highways. Here are birds singing, cows resting in peaceful pastures, and sunny days of riding, laughing, and playing with friends.

But, here, too, is the darker side of life during the Civil War, the rumors of General Lee's advances toward Gettysburg, the threat of his spies, who take supplies and horses from the Union farmers, the courage and heroism of the brave men and boys on the battlefield, and the women and girls who, like Kathleen, maintain the homefront routine.

Yet this story is more than a panoramic view of life during the Civil War. It is also a thrilling tale about a young girl who unwittingly becomes a traitor by befriending a Confederate spy! It is also a story of compassion and kindness, teaching us that, above all, in the Battle of Gettysburg there were no "winners," no "losers," only ordinary people dying for their beliefs.

When Alice Turner Curtis wrote her "Yankee Girl" series, the war had been over for only fifty years and its memories were still fresh in America. As a youngster, Curtis watched the schooners come and go from her coastline Massachusetts town, and her imagination gave birth to ideas that would later become her historical novels. As an adult, she wrote about what it was like for a young girl to grow up in the past during wartime, to witness real-life battles in a countryside that, days before, had been perfectly peaceful, and then, to stand tall while Abraham Lincoln gave his famous Gettysburg Address.

Join Alice Turner Curtis's heroine, the energetic, lively, and courageous Kathleen Webb, and travel back to a time and place that really existed, where historic events took shape, where young girls felt very much the way they do today, even so long ago and so very far away.

KARLA DOUGHERTY

Montclair, New Jersey
1995

KATHLEEN
A YANKEE GIRL
AT GETTYSBURG

CHAPTER 1

A BIRTHDAY VISIT

"ELEVEN YEARS OLD! Eleven years old!"

Kathleen Webb repeated these three words over and over to herself as she rode happily along the highway that led from her home to the town of Gettysburg. She tried to sit up as straight and tall as possible on the seat beside her father. Now and then she would look a little questioningly at his serious face and wonder if he could possibly have forgotten that this was the fifteenth day of April, and that his only daughter was now eleven years of age.

But of course he had not forgotten. Wasn't he taking her to Gettysburg as a special birthday treat to spend the day with Aunt Melvina Stevens? And remembering this delightful fact, Kathleen bounced up and down on the broad seat. Suddenly she clasped both hands about her father's arm and exclaimed: "Aunt Melvina always has birthday surprises! Last year it was this locket." Her clasp on her father's arm relaxed as she reached up to touch the small gold locket that swung on its slender chain around her neck. "And what do you suppose it will be today, Father?" Kathleen's blue eyes looked up at her father with such apparent delight that Mr. Webb smiled and for the moment forgot his own anxious thoughts.

"Who knows what Aunt Melvina has planned," he said. "But do not forget that you have a gift for her, and I am sure she will be pleased with it. You can tell your aunt that she can thank your Yankee grandmother for teaching you how to make a hooked rug."

"Is Grandma Webb a Yankee?" asked Kathleen, her thoughts flying back to the village on the Maine coast that had been her home until she was eight years old. Her Grandmother and Grandfather Webb still lived in Bloomville, Maine.

"Of course she is, and so are you, and so am I," declared her father. "If being a Yankee means loyalty to the United States," he added, as if to himself.

"Do you like Gettysburg as well as Bloomville, Father? Ted says there's not another town in Pennsylvania that is the center of a wheel!" Kathleen gave a little chuckle as she remembered her brother's drawing of the town, with its eleven different roads radiating from it like spokes of a wheel.

"Ted is right," replied Mr. Webb, his smile vanishing as he thought of the military importance of this peaceful town. It was the spring of 1863 and the Confederate Army was at the height of its military success. Mr. Webb recalled the rumors that the Confederates were considering an invasion of Pennsylvania. If such an invasion of a loyal state were carried out, what town could offer such a center as Gettysburg?

But he said nothing of these anxious thoughts to Kathleen, who was now looking toward the ridge at the west of the town, where the white cupola of the seminary rose clearly against the blue April sky.

The house of her Aunt Melvina Stevens was not far from the seminary, and Aunt Melvina had promised to take Kathleen to the cupola one day. From there, one could look for miles in every direction. Kathleen wondered if perhaps they could climb up the stairs this very day and look off toward South Mountain, the distant village of Cashtown, and down the wide turnpikes leading into Maryland. Kathleen decided to remind Aunt Melvina of her promise; wouldn't it be something to tell Mother and Ted about, she thought. Occupied with these pleasant thoughts of her birthday visit, Kathleen did not notice her father's silence, and when they came in sight of the square stone house near the slope leading to the top of the ridge, she called out, "Father, look! Aunt Melvina has the flag up because it is my birthday." Kathleen pointed to the Stars and Stripes waving over her aunt's house with the feeling that her birthday celebration was now really about to begin.

The Stevens house was built of fieldstone, with a big chimney at each end. The little windows in the roof always made Kathleen think of watchful eyes. The house stood quite near the road, but a stone wall, over which grew a tangle of vines and rose bushes, separated it from the street. Inside the wall were beds of tall yellow daffodils, now in full blossom, and lilac bushes budded for bloom; honeysuckle climbed the rough walls of the house, and woodbine and clematis trailed over the narrow porch.

Mr. Webb had not yet reached the gate when a woman came running down the footpath calling a lively welcome. Kathleen thought, as she often did when she saw her Aunt Melvina, that she did not look like an aunt; she looked like a grown-up girl. Indeed, Melvina Stevens, with her pleasant gray eyes, her smooth brown hair, and her cheerful readiness to smile, was, in spite of her thirty years, only a grown-up girl. She was Mrs. Webb's youngest sister and lived in the family home. Her two brothers, Kathleen's uncles, for whom she kept house, were with the Union Army, so now Melvina lived alone with two elderly servants.

"Aunty Mel! Aunty Mel!" called Kathleen. "I've brought you a rug! I made it myself! It's a surprise!" The little girl ran to meet her aunt, who exclaimed:

"Oh, you really are growing up," and she kissed the little girl six times on each cheek. "One kiss a year for luck, and an extra for pluck!" she said gaily. "And where is the rug? I can hardly wait to see it."

"Father is bringing it," replied Kathleen, as Mr. Webb came up the path carrying a long, neatly wrapped package. Inside was the hooked rug that Kathleen had made during the past winter.

As soon as they were indoors, Aunt Melvina untied the cords and spread the rug on the painted floor of the tiny front entry.

"It's a beauty!" she exclaimed.

"I drew the pattern myself," declared Kathleen. "See, Aunty Mel, it has a rose bush in the center, and the vine goes to each corner. I drew it with a bit of charcoal. I helped Mother fasten the burlap in the rug frame, and I did all the rest myself."

It was small wonder the little girl was proud of her handiwork: the background of the rug was a soft leaf green, the roses were a pale creamy yellow, and the vine was a deep green. The surface of the rug was smooth and even, and it was made of bits of woolen cloth, cut in tiny shreds and then drawn through the loosely woven burlap. Her Grandma Webb had first taught her little granddaughter how to hook a rug, when Kathleen was very small indeed.

"That's a Yankee rug!" Mr. Webb declared, smiling, but Melvina shook her head.

"Pennsylvania women can make them," she said.

"Well, Pennsylvanians are Yankees now, you know," said Mr. Webb as he followed Melvina and Kathleen into a square room at the end of the hall. "Coffee! And waffles!" he exclaimed approvingly as a stout elderly black woman came bustling into the room and set her tray on the table.

"And honey!" Melvina added, untying the broad white ribbon strings of Kathleen's pretty straw hat. They all seated themselves at the round table in the center of the room while Dosia, who had cheerily greeted Kathleen and Mr. Webb, poured the fragrant coffee, and served them some hot waffles.

"I must start home at once," said Mr. Webb as he finished his plate of waffles. "I promised Ted to help him with the wheat; the lad is a good farmer for a boy of fifteen, but he's getting uneasy, wants to be a soldier."

"All Pennsylvania boys now want to be soldiers, especially those whose fathers have fought," said Melvina. Mr. Webb had been wounded at Bull Run, and even now limped a little, although he often declared himself as well as ever.

While her father and aunt talked of Ted, of the possibility that General Robert E. Lee might lead his army, which seemed invincible, into Pennsylvania, Kathleen wandered about the sunny room. On a table in the corner she noticed a small package wrapped in white paper and tied with a pale blue cord. "That's for me! I'm sure it is. It's my birthday present! Oh, why doesn't Aunty Mel give it to me?" she thought, and suddenly it occurred to her that it would be a splendid joke on Aunt Mel to slip the little package into the pocket of her blue skirt and say nothing about it. "Then when Aunty is ready to give it to me she'll find it's gone! And then I'll say: 'Oh! Have you lost something?' " Kathleen found it difficult not to laugh aloud as she quickly slipped the package into her pocket.

"Well, good-bye, Kathleen. Your aunt will bring you home this afternoon, and maybe you will find a surprise at home," called her father. Kathleen ran down to the gate to watch him drive away.

"Now, my dear, come and see your present," said Aunt Mel, putting her arm around Kathleen's shoulders, and adding, "Oh, dear! Your hair is growing darker! It's almost copper color."

"Never mind," laughed Kathleen, shaking back her mass of wavy hair and wishing that her mother would permit her to have it cut short. "Never mind my hair. I want to see my present," and she wondered why Aunty Mel led her along the path toward the stable and barns instead of into the house.

"Do you need to speak to Uncle Job first?" she asked, seeing the old black man coming toward them, but before Aunt Melvina could reply, Kathleen had spotted a stout brown pony harnessed to a little brown cart with a high-backed seat. It was just the most adorable pony and cart, she thought. Who did it belong to? Did they have a visitor? Aunt Mel led Kathleen over to the brown pony.

"Here, Frisk! Look up; this is your new little mistress." Then Aunt Mel handed the white leather reins to her niece. "Kathleen, here is your birthday present."

CHAPTER 2

THE MISSING BOX

FOR A MOMENT Kathleen did not speak. She looked at the pony, at the reins in her hands, and then at Aunt Melvina, who was smiling as if it were she who had just received the most wonderful present that anyone could possibly imagine. Then Kathleen realized that her dearest wish had come true—that this fat, sleek brown pony in his shining harness, and this pretty cart with its high-backed seat, were really her very own. She dropped the white reins and flung her arms around her aunt, exclaiming, "Aunty Mel! Nobody thinks of such lovely things as you do! Oh! I never expected I would really ever have a pony." Kathleen had not really said "Thank you," but her aunt seemed very well pleased.

"Suppose you take me for a drive," suggested Aunt Melvina. "Frisk has not been exercised this morning, and I'd like to be the first who drives with you."

"Where will we go?" asked Kathleen as she took her seat beside her aunt. Uncle Job turned the pony's head toward the road and handed Kathleen the white reins.

"We could drive to Oak Ridge," suggested Aunt Melvina. Kathleen, who had often held the reins when riding with her father or Ted, now guided Frisk along the smooth turnpike leading to Oak Ridge. The seminary buildings could be clearly seen in the distance. Frisk trotted along at a good pace as if he enjoyed the warm spring air and the fragrance of plowed fields and budding flowers as much as Aunt Mel and Kathleen did. Kathleen's copper-colored hair blew back from her face, her blue eyes shone with happiness, and her cheeks were flushed with the pleasure of her wonderful birthday gift—Frisk. Aunt Mel's face glowed with satisfaction as she looked at her little niece. Surely, she thought, Kathleen was the dearest and prettiest girl in all Pennsylvania.

"Are we going straight to the seminary, Aunt Mel?" asked Kathleen as the road turned along the summit of the ridge.

"Why not? Would you like to go up to the cupola and look off toward South Mountain, and, for that matter, all over Gettysburg?" said Aunt Mel. "I think that is as far as we ought to drive without our hats, even if it is as warm as summer."

10

Kathleen promptly agreed. She would have liked to drive Frisk on and on, but it had long been one of her cherished wishes to climb to the top of this large building and see the view. She brought the pony to a standstill in the pleasant shade of a wide-spreading oak tree, where a stretch of grass ground bordered the highway.

"This is a good place to leave him, isn't it, Aunt Mel?" she asked. Aunt Melvina agreed that no place could be better and showed Kathleen how to fasten the pony's bridle rein to a fence pole. In a few moments they reached the entrance to the seminary and began climbing the stairs to the cupola.

"Everything splendid is happening to me today!" Kathleen declared. "First, and best, is my pony; but here am I almost at the top of the seminary, and—" Kathleen suddenly stopped, for they had reached the cupola, and there spread out before them like a beautiful picture lay the peaceful town of Gettysburg, with its gardens and shade trees and comfortable homes. Far above the treetops rose the South Mountain range, and nearer at hand a high granite spur projected above the dense growth of oaks and pines. This rocky spur was called Little Round Top, and Kathleen remembered that Ted had climbed it only the previous week.

A soft haze hung over the distant mountains, and the delicate greens of the young beech leaves, the deeper green of the dark pines, and here and there the silvery stems of a group of birches made up a picture that Kathleen always recalled when she thought of Gettysburg.

"I can see all the spokes of the wheel," she told Aunt Mel. "Ted says that Gettysburg is the hub and the eleven roads that center in the town are the spokes of a big wheel."

"Yes, and I hope the Southern Army does not realize that we are only seven miles from Maryland, with the best roads in the country," responded Aunt Melvina, for the moment forgetting that her companion was a young girl celebrating her eleventh birthday.

But at the mention of the Southern Army, Kathleen asked eagerly, "Would General Robert E. Lee come with the Southern Army if they invaded Pennsylvania?"

"Why, Kathleen! You sound as if you think it would be a fine thing for Gettysburg if General Lee and his army came marching upon us. And you a Yankee girl!" said Aunt Mel, smiling at Kathleen's serious face. "General Lee would surely come with his army, my dear. But we must hope he will be satisfied with his Virginia victories and not bring the war into Pennsylvania."

"Aunty Mel, I wish I could see General Lee! My father says he is the finest man in all the South," said Kathleen.

"Well, listen to that, and your father a Yankee soldier!" said her aunt. "But I hope you will not see the splendid Lee at present, dear child." Aunt Mel's face again grew serious as she looked at the misty range of South Mountain.

Kathleen turned her glance toward a distant peach orchard, but at that moment she made herself a promise—a promise that before the summer ended was to bring her into great peril. "If General Lee does come to Gettysburg, I'll see him," Kathleen told herself, not realizing that the invasion of Southern armies would mean a terrible battle, and perhaps the defeat of the Northern forces.

"We must not keep Frisk waiting too long," said Aunt Mel as she clasped Kathleen by the hand and drew the little girl toward the stairway. "And there's another birthday surprise," she added. At this Kathleen suddenly remembered the little package that she had taken from the table and slipped into her own pocket. For a moment she was tempted to tell her aunt of the joke she had planned, but Aunty Mel was again speaking: "I think I must tell you that the next surprise is company for your birthday dinner."

"Oh, Aunty Mel! Is it Beth and Janet?" Kathleen asked eagerly, and at her aunt's smiling nod she exclaimed happily: "Oh! Everything lovely is happening today! I do wish every day was a birthday!"

"But you'd be a hundred years old before you knew it," laughed Aunt Mel as she took her seat beside the happy girl. Kathleen now urged the pony to trot quickly toward home, thinking that Beth and Janet were sure to admire Frisk. She planned to let each one of them drive the pony one day.

Beth and Janet Ross were twin sisters who lived not far from the Stevens farm. Unlike many twins they did not look much alike, for Beth was chubby and Janet thin. They had just turned ten, and they were the only girls that Kathleen knew well enough to think of as real friends. Beth and Janet were not as fortunate as Kathleen. Their father had been killed at Bull Run, and their mother was doing her best to manage, but there was no extra money to buy Beth and Janet the pretty hats, dresses, and many luxuries that Kathleen's parents could so easily afford. All this flashed through Kathleen's thoughts as she turned Frisk into the driveway. Uncle Job met them at the stable. "We had such a wonderful ride," said Kathleen. Then she patted Frisk's brown head and followed her aunt indoors.

Dosia came hurrying to say that the company had arrived. Kathleen ran to greet the two girls, who stood smiling in the open doorway. "Happy birthday!" they cried, and Beth handed her a package, saying: "We made it for you, Kathleen!" Kathleen thanked them enthusiastically, thinking she would ask her mother to invite Beth and Janet to visit at the Webb farm. "Why don't you look at our present, Kathleen?" said Janet, and they all laughed because

Kathleen was holding the square package as carefully as if it were glass.

She took off the paper in which it was wrapped, and exclaimed with pleasure at the pretty box. At first glance it looked like a pine cone, but Kathleen was quick to see that it was made of wood, with the small petals of pine cones cleverly fastened on, one overlapping another, just as on a pine cone.

"Mother showed us how to make it," Janet explained, as she lifted the pointed end of the cone-shaped box. "Beth made the wooden part from a piece of old cedar. See, Kathleen, she cut out the center bit by bit with a sharp knife, and then made the cover. Isn't it smooth?" Janet studied the inside of the box admiringly.

"But it was Janet who stuck on the cone petals. Mother told her how to do it," Beth explained. "We thought you could keep your locket and chain and your pearl beads in it," she added, a little questioningly. Kathleen quickly responded that the cone box would be exactly right to hold such treasures, and she again thanked the twins for making it for her.

"I'll always keep it," she promised, "and when I go back to Maine I'll have it to remember you by."

"But you are not going back to Maine, are you, Kathleen?" Beth questioned anxiously. "I thought your father and mother were going to live here always."

"Oh, I guess we'll go back sometime," said Kathleen, who often made plans for a surprise visit to Grandpa and Grandma Webb.

The twins had seen Frisk on his arrival on the previous day, and they quickly agreed with Kathleen that he was all a pony could possibly be in beauty, good temper, and swiftness.

"I want to ride horseback," said Kathleen. "I know Father will get me a saddle, and when you come to visit me you shall both ride." The twins happily declared that they hoped they could soon visit the Webb farm.

Aunt Melvina had left the little girls by themselves, but she now came to call them to dinner. They followed her into the dining room where Kathleen and her father had eaten waffles only a few hours earlier.

It was a real birthday dinner, with roast duckling and jelly, sweet potatoes and corn pancakes, and slender glasses filled with grape juice. And then the door into the kitchen opened and in came Dosia holding up a round blue plate. On the plate stood a cake covered with heavy white frosting; across the top of the cake, in heavy pink sugar letters, was the name "Kathleen," and just below it the figure "11."

Kathleen cut the cake with the wide bladed silver knife that Dosia handed her. In Janet's piece there was a finely engraved gold ring; Beth's piece held a pretty silver thimble, and Aunt Mel found a shoe button in her cake, but Kathleen had nothing at all.

Kathleen was just thinking that she would give the other half of the big cake to Beth and Janet, to take home to their mother, when her aunt said: "Dosia, there is a little package on the corner table. Please bring it to me." Then, with a smile at her young guests, she added, "This isn't another present for Kathleen; it is something for you, my dears," and she nodded at Beth and Janet.

"There's no package on this table," declared Dosia. And as she spoke Kathleen reached into her pocket, planning to draw out the box and say: "Here it is, Aunt Mel." Her hand went down and down, but there was no box there!

"Aunty Mel!" she exclaimed aloud, and she was about to tell of the joke she had planned and how the box was now lost. But Aunt Mel jumped up from the table, saying, "Why, it must be there! I put it there myself just as Kathleen arrived this morning. I am sure no one would touch it." Then she hurried to the table to make sure that Dosia had not overlooked it, and now Kathleen felt that she could not tell her aunt that she had taken the present intended for Beth and Janet and lost it.

"I must find the box, then I'll tell her," she decided, as Aunt Mel at last agreed that Dosia was right, that there was no box on the table.

"I'll run upstairs and look on my table," she said with another smile at Beth and Janet, who were looking at each other with such clear disappointment that Kathleen felt more guilty than before. Without a word she ran out of the room toward the stable, for she had suddenly thought that the box might have dropped on the floor of the pony cart.

CHAPTER 3

PAYING A DEBT

THE BOX WAS NOT to be found, and when Kathleen again checked her pocket she discovered a hole that the package could easily have slipped through. She was back in the dining room before her aunt came downstairs, and Beth and Janet, somewhat to Kathleen's surprise, did not seem greatly disappointed by the disappearance of the present intended for them.

"Do you think your mother would let you both visit me?" Kathleen asked, thinking that she must find out what had been in the package and try to give Beth and Janet something exactly like it.

"Perhaps," Beth responded. "When would you like us to come?"

"I'd like you to come for May Day and stay all night!" declared Kathleen. "You ask your mother and let me know!"

"Let's go ask her now, and you come with us. It won't take a minute!" suggested Janet eagerly, and a

19

moment later Aunt Melvina looked out her window and saw the three girls racing down the road.

"We never went on a visit in all our life," said Janet as they reached the Ross's cottage, where Kathleen asked Mrs. Ross whether Beth and Janet could come out to the Webb farm for a May Day visit.

"Ted and I will come pick them up," Kathleen promised. Mrs. Ross said the twins could go, and seemed nearly as pleased as the girls themselves. As Kathleen and her friends ran back to Aunt Melvina's, they began making plans for all they would do when May Day came. Kathleen almost forgot that she was to blame for the lost package, and when Aunty Mel announced that the box could not be found, Kathleen exclaimed, "Never mind! I'm going to plan a present for Beth and Janet." She wondered why Aunty Mel was smiling with such approval.

The two weeks between Kathleen's birthday and the day set for her friends' visit passed quickly. She now rode Frisk all over the paths and roads near the farm and had twice driven her mother into Gettysburg. It had been decided, however, that Aunt Melvina would bring Janet and Beth to the farm, and on the day set for their arrival, Kathleen was unusually busy. As soon as she ate her breakfast, she ran upstairs and looked into the room where Beth and Janet were to sleep. It was just across the hall from Kathleen's room, and its windows looked out over beautiful fields and orchards toward Rock Creek.

Kathleen gave a little exclamation of delight as she stood in the doorway and saw the two beds: What caught her eye was not the smooth beds with their tufted spreads and lace-trimmed pillows, nor the ruffled muslin curtains at the windows, the shining pumpkin yellow of the painted floor with its pretty homemade rugs, or any of the furnishings of the room. The room was really very much like her own. But on each bed in this room lay a white muslin dress, "like white clouds," thought Kathleen as she gazed admiringly at the fluffy lace-trimmed skirts and then at the wide ruffled sash next to each dress.

These white dresses were Kathleen's May Day presents to her friends. Her mother and aunt had been surprised by Kathleen's insistence that these were really to be her gifts to Beth and Janet, and Mrs. Webb had allowed Kathleen to empty her tin bank to pay for the fabric. Kathleen had even helped to make the dresses. Each day, sitting beside her mother, she had hemmed ruffles and taken out basting threads as if there were no better fun in all the world. And now, as she looked at the pretty gowns, she gave a little chuckle and told herself that, no matter what Aunt Mel had put in that lost package, it could not have been prettier than these dresses.

"But I wish Aunty Mel would tell me what her present was just the same." Kathleen was never quite comfortable thinking about that lost package, but today, looking at her gifts for the twins, she felt happier than she had since her birthday. Her glance turned to the dresser, where she had put a blue bowl filled with wild lilies and ferns and violets that she had gathered the previous day. Everything was ready to welcome her friends, so Kathleen ran back to the kitchen where her mother was busy helping Hitty, Dosia's daughter, who was just taking a cake from the oven. Hitty looked over her shoulder to smile at Kathleen and say, "I'll bet your company never tasted a better cake than this one! Eleven eggs, a pound of butter, a pound of—" but Kathleen did not wait to hear the rest of the recipe. She went over to the window where her mother was using a big silver spoon to beat up a white frothy mixture, which Kathleen knew was the frosting for the big cake.

"Mother, could you make letters out of sugar? Could you make a *B* and a *J?* Could you, Mother?" She looked so anxiously into her mother's face that Mrs. Webb again wondered why Kathleen wanted to do so much for the Ross girls, but she just smiled and replied that she was quite sure she could make letters of sugar for the top of the cake.

"And will you, Mother dear? Will you? And may I tell Beth and Janet that it is their own special cake? Aunt Mel says that Mrs. Ross cannot afford cakes!" she added. Mrs. Webb was happy to promise that this particular cake should be what Kathleen called Beth and Janet's "special cake."

Having made sure of this, Kathleen put on her wide-rimmed straw hat and ran off to the pasture, where Frisk was quietly feeding. She did not stop near the pony but headed on to the spring that bubbled up at the foot of a steep ledge, well out of sight of the house. Tall ferns grew just above it, and nearby a bed of white violets flourished. As Kathleen knelt and began to pick the delicate blossoms, a brown partridge whirred up and staggered clumsily into the underbrush, dragging a wing as if it were broken.

"I know all about *you*," Kathleen called. "You are just making believe so I won't find your young chicks! Oh, here they come!" and a dozen little round partridge chicks came huddling together, then vanished just where the mother partridge had disappeared.

Sitting back on her heels, Kathleen looked up at the steep ledge and then at the thick growth of pine trees that stretched toward the brook. She smiled happily as she thought of the two May baskets that she had made on the previous day. She planned to hang them on the door to Beth and Janet's room.

She had made the baskets of strips of birch bark cleverly braided together, with handles of supple young willow twigs. She would fill the baskets with feathery green moss and white violets.

"I ought to write a verse for each basket," she told herself, "something about how glad I am that they are here for May Day." Various rhymes began to sing through Kathleen's thoughts as she climbed the ledge to the mossy spot where she had left her May baskets. She began to fill them with damp moss and flowers.

She had been there only a few moments when the sound of voices close at hand made her look quickly about, but she was so shut in by the ledge on one side and by a growth of dogwood on the other that she could not see, or be seen by, anyone, and she did not recognize the voice that was speaking: "I tell you Gettysburg is as easily captured as if it had been designed for the Southern Army to take it. And from here General Lee can move on to Washington, Baltimore, even to Philadelphia—in a word, conquer the Northern Army on their own soil."

Kathleen held her breath as she listened eagerly for the response.

"Don't speak so loud; there's a house not far off, and some workman or child may be near," she heard, and then the first voice answered, "No fear of that; this ledge is straight up and down on the sides toward the farm. I reckon General Lee has his plans to make a big move before long, perhaps to Harrisburg. His army is ready for anything, while the Yanks have been beaten so many times they have lost courage."

"Don't be too sure of that" came the quick response. "General Hooker is brave enough, and with Hancock and Meade at hand the fight might not be too easy. But we'd best be moving on. I have a map of all the general will need to know about this part of the country." Kathleen heard a scrambling movement toward the top of the ledge and knew that the men were gone.

"Lee's scouts," the little girl whispered to herself, forgetting all about her May baskets and Janet and Beth's visit. For in the spring of 1863, children as well as their elders knew how serious and terrible the war between North and South was. This conflict would determine whether the United States remained an undivided nation, as the North believed it should, or was cut in two, as the South believed right. If Lee and his Southern armies continued their triumphs, slavery would continue, while if the Northern armies won, black people could no longer be bought and sold.

Something of all this flashed through Kathleen's thoughts as, leaving her baskets behind her, she crept noiselessly toward the spring. For a moment she stood perfectly still, listening. But there was no unfamiliar sound, and she realized that the men who had stopped to rest among the rocks and bushes of the ledge were now out of sight in the thick, tall pine forest that stretched off toward the Maryland border.

"I must tell my father," she decided, and ran swiftly across the pastures to the field where her father and Ted were at work.

Mr. Webb's face grew anxious as he listened to Kathleen's breathless story of the conversation she had overheard, and Ted was eager to start off at once and try to capture the Confederate scouts. But Mr.

Webb shook his head. "It couldn't be done. The men are miles away by now, but it is fortunate Kathleen overheard what she did. I'll let the men of Gettysburg know what's being said and that there is no doubt that General Lee plans to bring the war into Pennsylvania."

Kathleen listened to every word. If this great general of the Southern forces, a man beloved by his own men and deeply respected by his Northern opponents, really came near her home, perhaps, she thought hopefully, she might see him. She could not even imagine the terrible results of such an invasion, and when she turned toward home Kathleen pictured to herself a fine soldierly man who would smile upon her in a friendly way. That, indeed, was exactly what General Lee was to do before Kathleen's next birthday.

Aunt Melvina brought Beth and Janet Ross to the Webb farm early in the afternoon. Mrs. Webb had warned Kathleen not to mention her morning's adventure, so nothing was said of the menace of advancing armies that might soon sweep over this peaceful countryside. In the excitement of welcoming Beth and Janet, who had never visited her before, Kathleen forgot all about her father's anxiety and her own wish to see General Robert Lee. She led Beth and Janet to their room, eager to see their reaction to the pretty white muslin dresses.

Kathleen could see that the dresses worn by the twins had faded from blue to a dull white. Their well-polished shoes had been mended, and their hats were the same ones they had worn all winter, but neither Beth nor Janet seemed to be thinking about what they wore. They were bubbling over with delight to be visiting the Webb farm, and they accepted the muslin dresses with so much admiration that Kathleen jumped about the room as if she were a frisky kitten instead of an eleven-year-old girl. It was not until almost suppertime that a small shadow fell upon her pleasure. The three girls were all talking happily about the May Day picnic planned for the coming day, when Beth exclaimed, "Oh, Kathleen! We know now what was in the little box that was lost on your birthday, the box Miss Mel was going to give to Janet and me!"

Kathleen waited. She could not even ask what that lost package held, but instantly Beth went on: "You never could guess, and Miss Mel doesn't know that we know, but we do. Dosia told us. Kathleen! Just think, there were two five-dollar gold pieces in that box: one for Janet and one for me. Isn't it too bad they were lost!" Kathleen's exclamation convinced the twins that she was as sorry about it as they could possibly be.

CHAPTER 4

VISITORS

KATHLEEN DID HER best not to let Beth and Janet see that she was so upset about the lost box. She told herself that being sorry was not enough; if she could not find that box then she must see to it that Beth and Janet each received a five-dollar gold piece. Glancing toward her friends she again noticed how worn and shabby their dresses and shoes were. Kathleen had to fight a rush of tears as she realized that the lost gold pieces would have bought new shoes and hats for both Janet and Beth.

But how ever could she find an excuse to go searching for the missing box at the cupola of the seminary, where, she began to feel sure, it must have fallen from her pocket? And if it was not to be found, how ever could an eleven-year-old girl earn ten dollars?

"Rugs!" Kathleen suddenly exclaimed so that Beth and Janet stared at her in amazement. Kathleen quickly added, "Come and see the rug I am making," and hurried them through the sitting room to a long narrow room whose windows looked out toward the meadows and ledge and distant forest.

This room was Kathleen's schoolroom, workroom, and playhouse. Beth's round face beamed with interest as she glanced from the bookshelves to a big globe of the world, while Janet's hazel eyes shone with pleasure as she discovered the frame holding the burlap foundation for the rug Kathleen was at work on.

"Isn't it splendid to go to school at home? I wish we could," said Beth, resting both hands on the low solid table holding the globe.

"Oh, Beth! Think of all the fun we have at recess with the other girls! And singing, too! And even staying after school when Miss Smith talks to us in fun!" Janet eagerly declared. But Beth shook her curly head in disagreement, and Kathleen for the time forgot about the lost gold pieces. She helped Beth discover Africa on the globe, and China and Japan, and pointed out New England, where her Grandma Webb lived. In answer to Beth's eager questions, Kathleen told them just how she "went to school at home."

"Mother and I read stories about history," she said, "about little girls in far-off times who knew kings and queens and brave soldiers. And I learn a poem every week, and I draw pictures, and Ted and I work out games out of an arithmetic book."

"Arithmetic isn't a game; it's addition and subtraction and multiplication and division and fractions!" declared Beth, but Kathleen laughed delightedly.

"It's games, just the same! Puzzles and games that you work out with figures," she said, "and every day I write a letter to my Grandma Webb, though I only send them once a week. And I go on journeys around the globe! That's fun! I start at Gettysburg and go to New York and take a steamer for Constantinople." Kathleen spun the globe and pointed out some of her travels to the surprised twins. Even Janet began to think that, after all, there was much to be said for the way Kathleen went to school.

They all gathered about the rug and admired its pattern. Kathleen had drawn a small pine tree in the center, and in each corner was a branch of pine. "It is to be all green, different shades," she explained. "Hitty dyed a lot of pieces for me. And she said the rug would be worth five dollars. I could make two rugs and that would be ten dollars," she added thoughtfully.

"Who would you sell them to?" questioned Beth.

But before Kathleen could consider this puzzling question, Hitty appeared in the doorway.

"Your supper's all ready, Miss Kathie," she announced, and Kathleen's thoughts fled to the big "special" cake that was to surprise Beth and Janet. She hurried the girls to the dining room, where Aunty

Mel, in a silvery gray gown, Mrs. Webb, Mr. Webb, and Ted were all waiting for them. But it was Kathleen who was more surprised than Beth and Janet, for the windows were wreathed with vines and dogwood blossoms, and the table seemed to be set in a blossoming arbor. Kathleen exclaimed in delight. Aunt Melvina, Mrs. Webb, and Ted had been at work ever since Aunt Mel's arrival setting up a light framework that Mr. Webb had made to enclose the table. The framework was wreathed with branches of lilacs and dogwood blossoms, and Kathleen was sure that nothing could be more lovely than this supper table spread so abundantly.

Ted welcomed his sister's friends with a smile. He looked so much like Kathleen that both Beth and Janet felt instantly acquainted with the tall boy who so politely drew their chairs back from the table for them.

Everyone enjoyed the excellent supper. Then the cake was brought in, and Kathleen teasingly asked Beth and Janet to tell her what the big pink sugar *B* and *J* stood for. When the twins realized that it was their own special cake, they smiled so radiantly that everyone else at the table smiled in response, and it seemed to Kathleen that her Aunt Mel looked at her with even more approval than usual. But as they all left the table, Aunt Mel put her arm about Kathleen and whispered, "I know why you are trying to do so much for Janet and Beth; it's because you are sorry about the lost box!" Kathleen fairly gasped in astonishment and dismay, for she was sure her aunt knew that she had taken the box and lost it, but before she could stammer out that she had taken it in fun, Aunt Mel's soft voice continued: "But I believe I'll find it yet. It must be in the house. Didn't you see it on the table?"

"Mel, come in the sitting room," called Mrs. Webb, and without waiting for Kathleen's reply, Aunt Melvina hurried away. Kathleen followed her brother and the twins outside, where Ted decided to show the girls some horseback tricks. He led his little gray horse out of the stable, saying: "I have trained Patch myself, and he knows every word I say, don't you, Patch?" His horse, named for the patches of black on his shoulders, bowed his head and whinnied in response. Then Ted sprang lightly onto Patch's back, and without curb or bridle, balancing himself first on one foot and then on the other, sent the horse cantering around the yard.

"I'm going to teach Frisk all these things," declared Kathleen, after Patch, at Ted's command, had bowed and offered his right forehoof to each girl and then trotted obediently off to graze.

"Oh, I guess not!" laughed Ted. "Frisk is too old to learn tricks. He's two years old, and I began to teach Patch before he was three months old."

But Kathleen and Beth were both confident that it would be an easy matter to teach the pony to bow and offer his forefoot in greeting. Beth was sure that she could ride standing on the pony's fat back, and Kathleen promised they would give the pony his first lesson on the following morning.

They were all turning back to the house when the sound of a galloping horse made them look toward the highway. "That's a Union soldier," said Ted. "I can see the blue coat." A moment later the horseman stopped directly in front of the gate where the children were standing and asked: "Is this the best road to Gettysburg?"

"As good as any of the others, sir," Ted answered. He hoped the stranger would ask him to explain more about the roads leading into Gettysburg, but Mr. Webb came hurrying toward the gate and urged the stranger to dismount and rest.

"We are celebrating May Day eve, and supper is still on the table. I am sure these girls want you to taste a fine frosted cake," said Mr. Webb to the stranger. "My name is Webb, and that I have recently finished my service with the Northern Army."

The soldier responded that his name was Mason, and that he would be glad of rest and refreshment. As Mason walked to the house with Mr. Webb, Ted led the tired horse to the stable.

Kathleen and the twins followed Mr. Webb and the soldier into the dining room, and the girls smiled at the stranger's exclamation of surprise and admiration over the flower-decked room. He was clearly very tired, and when Mrs. Webb came to welcome him with a hot cup of tea, suggesting that Hitty could whip up an omelette, the young man declared that he was ashamed to make trouble when he was hungry enough to eat anything.

Kathleen ran to the kitchen to bring in a plate of freshly baked biscuits, while Beth and Janet seated themselves near one of the windows. Kathleen soon joined them, and the three girls whispered together over their May Day plans until the soldier's story caught their interest. He had stopped to visit his home in Philadelphia, and now he was on his way to join the Army of the Potomac, which was in May of 1863, camped on the northern side of the Rappahannock River. On the southern side of the river, the Confederate Army of Northern Virginia, behind a strong line of earthworks, appeared to be idle, although in reality it was preparing for a tremendous effort against its enemy.

The young soldier said that Lee had a force of seventy thousand men—"men of the finest quality who have proved their mettle, and commanded by the finest of officers," he added. Mr. Webb agreed, even though he himself had fought in the Northern Army. The North had entered the war to defend the integrity of the Union and the supremacy of the Constitution, and to set free the slaves, but Mr. Webb recognized the nobility of the Southern men who were equally sure of their right to divide the nation into a Northern and a Southern Republic. On each side was perfect faith in their leaders and in the justice of their cause.

Mr. Webb told his visitor of Kathleen's adventure that morning when she had overheard the conversation of the Confederate scouts on the ledge. The young soldier was greatly interested and asked Kathleen to repeat exactly what the men had said. As he listened his face grew a little troubled.

"I am sure this news is valuable, of great importance," he declared, "and I shall be sure it reaches headquarters as soon as possible." As he spoke the young soldier rose to his feet, thanking the Webbs for their hospitality. Just before leaving the room, he turned and held out his hand to Kathleen, saying, "I wish I had been the one to hear those scouts declare that Lee planned to enter Pennsylvania. I'd like to tell General Buford of capturing them, but you can be sure he shall hear that a young Gettysburg girl told me."

"And do you think General Lee will really come here?" questioned Kathleen. At the soldier's answer: "Do not be afraid; if Lee comes the Union Army will be here to meet him," Kathleen's smile vanished, and Mr. Webb, resting his hand on his daughter's arm, said, "My little girl cannot realize what a terrible misfortune it would be for Lee to invade Pennsylvania. She thinks of him as a wonderful soldier, a fine hero, riding at the head of a wonderful army."

"Well, he is all that," declared the young Union officer. "Nevertheless I hope he'll keep out of Pennsylvania."

They all stood at the gate to watch the soldier ride away as the spring twilight deepened into darkness. The adults grew silent as they considered the possibility that before the summer ended terrible warfare might enter their state. But none of them could even dream that the hills and fields of Gettysburg were to be the scene of a conflict that would give the name historic immortality.

Kathleen suddenly remembered her May baskets abandoned among the ferns at the foot of the ledge. She would have to wake up early to fetch them and hang them on the door of the twins' room so they would be discovered the first thing on May Day morning. She decided to write the verses for the baskets before going to bed.

Beth did not notice the silence of her companions, for she was busy with her own thoughts. She would get up the next morning before anyone else in the house: then she could go to the pasture and practice riding Frisk as she had seen Ted ride Patch.

"I may never have another chance," thought Beth, "and there's no harm in riding Frisk. Kathleen said we could, but I'd rather ride without anybody seeing me the first time. When she sees how well I ride standing up on the pony's back, I guess she'll be surprised, and then I'll tell her about getting up early to practice."

Absorbed in their plans, neither Kathleen nor Beth noticed that Janet was smiling to herself as she walked slowly beside them. She, too, was thinking of something very pleasant indeed, for Janet as well as Kathleen and Beth had come up with a plan for early rising on May Day morning. Janet's plan, as it turned out, was to seriously surprise Ted and interfere with his most cherished scheme.

CHAPTER 5

MAY DAY

KATHLEEN WAS PLEASED with the verses that she finally wrote neatly on small squares of paper that she planned to fasten to the May baskets. On one paper she wrote: "To Janet Ross," and directly beneath it were these lines:

> *"Here is a basket for Janet;*
> *The prettiest one that I've made yet.*
> *With it I send*
> *The best of good wishes*
> *From your true friend."*

Under Beth's name she had written:

> *"May Day flowers and wishes, too;*
> *The best of everything I wish you.*
> *May all Beth's May Days happy be*
> *And every one be spent with me."*

"It would be splendid if I could only put a five-dollar gold piece in each basket," Kathleen thought, a little sadly, as she remembered how long it would take to make two hooked rugs. Making the rugs and finding a purchaser now seemed the only way she could ever earn the money to replace the coins in the lost box. More than once Kathleen had firmly resolved to tell Aunt Mel exactly what had happened. She was sure that her aunt would have understood if Kathleen had told her the moment she discovered the loss of the box, but so much time had now passed that Kathleen didn't want to say anything until she could either find the box, or have two bright gold pieces for the Ross twins. "Then I will explain about it," she promised herself, for she knew she would feel troubled until she had confessed to Aunt Mel.

Before she went to sleep she decided to do her best to persuade her mother to let her go home with Aunt Mel the very next day. Once she was within driving distance of the seminary, thought Kathleen, it would be easy to search for the box.

"And maybe I'll find it," she said to herself. Then she went to sleep without even a thought of armies, scouts, or soldiers, or of the possibility of General Robert E. Lee's appearance in Gettysburg.

When Beth awoke on May Day morning, the tall clock that stood in the front hallway was striking five, and the spring sunshine filled the room. In a moment Beth was out of bed. She peered anxiously across the room to make sure that she had not awakened Janet, but when Beth saw her sister's bed she exclaimed in surprise, "Where is she?" Janet was nowhere in the room.

"Oh, I'll bet she and Kathleen have a secret," thought the puzzled girl. "Perhaps it's May baskets, or perhaps they're teaching Frisk." Wishing that she had awakened even earlier, Beth dressed hurriedly and crept down the stairs to find the front door wide open. As she ran along the path behind the tall lilac bushes she could hear Aunt Hitty vigorously at work in the kitchen.

"Oh, dear! It isn't so early after all," she thought, looking toward the stable yard a little anxiously. But there was no one to be seen there. She ran toward the pasture beyond the stable, where yesterday she had seen the pony, but he was not there. Then Beth cautiously entered the stable. Instantly the pony whinnied a welcome and stretched his brown head out over the door of his roomy stall. Beth ran to him and stroked his head, feeding him the bits of sugar that she had taken from last night's supper table.

Frisk seemed as pleased to see his visitor as Beth had been to discover him, and he was clearly eager to get out in the sunshine.

"Yes, Frisk, just wait a minute and I'll let you out," Beth promised. After a quick glance to make sure that no one was coming, she reached up and drew back the stout bar that held the stall door.

"Come out, Frisk," she said, expecting the pony to walk out quietly and wait for her to grasp his mane and lead him wherever she wanted him to go. When Frisk instead darted out, kicking up his heels in delight at his freedom, the surprised girl stepped backward and stumbled over an empty bucket. She found herself lying on her back on the stable floor while Frisk raced about the stable yard. With no one there to interfere, the pony began to run down the road. By the time Beth had scrambled to her feet and reached the yard, Frisk was dashing along the highway. Beth, frightened and surprised, fled after him, calling, "Frisk! Frisk! Oh, I must catch him!"

Beth could not run very fast, but she did her best and managed to keep the brown pony in sight until a turn in the road hid him from view. At first this did not alarm her, but when she reached the curve and looked along the gray stretch of highway, the brown pony had disappeared.

"He's resting!" Beth told herself. She no longer ran at her top speed but walked hopefully on, looking from side to side of the wide roadway and expecting to discover Frisk feeding contentedly. How she would capture or control the pony after finding him did not even occur to Beth as she trudged sturdily on, and she had long since forgotten to wonder what had become of her missing sister, Janet.

Janet had been the earliest riser at the Webb farm on that May Day morning. She was awake a full hour before Beth and had dressed and left the house so quietly that no one even heard her. Janet's secret plan was not unlike her sister's. Janet, too, wanted to take her first riding lesson without anyone watching, only she decided it would be easier to ride Patch, as the little gray horse seemed so friendly and quiet. She could practice on Patch, thought Janet, and then surprise Kathleen and Beth with her skill on the pony. It did not occur to either of the twins that there was any possible harm in the plan that each, unknown to the other, had made. Janet ran along the grassy path behind the lilac bushes, smiling happily over the success of her plan, and nearly bumped right into the little gray horse. Saddled and bridled with an army knapsack fastened to his saddlebow, Patch stood quietly hidden in the thick bushes.

"My word!" exclaimed the surprised girl, looking quickly about, quite sure that Ted must be close at hand. But she saw no one. The early morning was cool and shadowy, and Janet shivered a little in her cotton dress. She patted the gray horse, and now

43

wondered if someone had meant to steal Patch. "Maybe I frightened them away," she thought hopefully, and then decided that it would not do to let Patch remain hidden behind the lilacs. She untied his bridle rein and led the well-trained horse down the little slope toward a big stump. "I can stand on the stump," thought Janet, "and then mount Patch." This proved as easy as she had expected, and she settled herself on the saddle, gathered up the reins, and laughed aloud. Surely there could be nothing more splendid than to be seated on Patch and have the whole world to herself.

In her satisfaction, Janet kicked her heels sharply against the horse's sides. To Patch those kicks had a definite meaning: he had been taught that two sharp kicks meant "Jump!" and as there was a low stone wall bordering the highway just in front of him, Patch cleared it at a bound. Then, feeling the reins tighten—for Janet clutched them frantically—he took off at a great pace.

Ted showed up just in time to see his horse racing down the highway. The astonished boy rushed angrily down the slope in pursuit, but it was too late for Patch or Janet to hear his shouts. The frightened Janet had dropped the reins and was clinging to Patch's mane and saddle in order to keep on his back.

"It's one of those girls!" muttered Ted, running after his horse. "I hope she'll stick on, the little fool!

What is she doing out at this hour? Some May Day trick, I suppose." Ted forgot for a moment that this unexpected turn of events would likely spoil his own plan to sneak out and join the Union Army. For after the departure of their soldier guest, the boy had made up his mind to run away. The soldier had said that the Northern Army needed more troops, that it had been defeated in a number of important battles and its men were losing courage. Ted, feeling himself nearly a man at fifteen, felt as so many boys did in 1863, boys of the South *and* boys of the North, that he wanted to fight for the right. To Ted Webb of Gettysburg, Pennsylvania, the right meant the freedom of the slaves, and an undivided nation, to be won only by the success of the Northern Army. Ted had packed a few belongings in his father's knapsack before he went to bed. This morning he had crept out while it was still dark, saddled Patch, and, if Janet had only slept a half hour longer, the boy would have made a good start and possibly carried out his plan.

But now, as he raced along hoping to get near enough to Patch for the well-trained horse to hear his voice, Ted was ready to cry with anger and disappointment. He realized that his attempt to run away from home and join the Northern Army was ruined, for his father had refused, months earlier, to give Ted permission for such an undertaking.

Now, what was Kathleen doing while her guests were busy getting themselves into trouble? Kathleen had awakened later than any of the other adventurous early risers, although she happily believed herself to be the first one awake, except Hitty, of course. Kathleen was convinced that Hitty was always up before sunrise, and when Kathleen now appeared in the kitchen, Hitty raised both hands in wonder as she exclaimed, "Whatever got you up at this hour?" Kathleen explained about the May baskets and her plan to hang them on the door of the twins' room. "I'll read you the verses I've written," she added, and Hitty listened with occasional exclamations of admiring praise as Kathleen read the May Day verses.

"Those are grand poems, Miss Kathy!" she declared solemnly. "Now you can have some of this porridge before you go out." Kathleen eagerly tasted the hot oatmeal and cream that Hitty offered her.

This kitchen visit, however, had delayed her, so that when Kathleen finally started for the ledge the sun was well up and she knew she had no time to lose. The twins would be coming downstairs before long.

She found her baskets among the ferns, the violets still fresh in the damp moss. Fastening the verses to the baskets, she headed back to the house and found her father and mother standing in the kitchen doorway.

"I'm going to hang these baskets on the door of the twins' room," Kathleen explained, holding up the flower-filled baskets, sure that her father and mother would admire them.

"But where are the twins?" asked Mrs. Webb. "Their door is wide open and they are not in their room. I thought they were with you."

CHAPTER 6

ADELAIDE MARY

WHEN IT WAS DISCOVERED that Ted, Patch and Frisk, as well as Janet and Beth, had disappeared, Mr. and Mrs. Webb decided that it must be some sort of a May morning celebration planned by Ted as a surprise for the Ross girls.

"Ted has evidently taken them for a morning ride, and they will all have fine appetites for breakfast. I think, Hitty, it will be a good plan to make an extra pan of popovers," said Mrs. Webb as she and Kathleen, May baskets in hand, walked to the front of the house.

"I think Ted should have taken me, too," said Kathleen, starting up the stairs with her flower-filled baskets. "Frisk is *my* pony, and I think Ted had no business to take him off this way. And Janet and Beth are *my* company!" declared Kathleen, disappointed at being completely left out of this early celebration of May Day. For the moment Kathleen forgot all her plans to do everything possible for the Ross twins. She was angry at Ted and did not even hear her mother's response as she ran to her room.

For a moment Kathleen considered destroying the pretty baskets and tearing up the carefully written verses. There were tears in her blue eyes as she turned toward the corner of her room and whispered, "Well, Adelaide Mary, I like you better than any girl there is, even if I am eleven years old and you are only a doll." Kathleen lifted a huge doll from a small wooden rocking-chair. Adelaide Mary had journeyed all the way from Maine in Kathleen's arms, but that was four years ago, and for the past year Kathleen had not been as interested in playing with her cherished doll, whose big china head had black painted ringlets, red cheeks, and blue eyes.

Adelaide Mary was dressed in a gown of green plaid silk, with white leather slippers, and she wore a tiny round hat ringed with little flowers. Kathleen had made everything that Adelaide Mary wore. As she lifted the doll, in spite of feeling hurt and angry at Ted, a little smile crept over her face and she whispered, "*You* never do hateful things, Adelaide Mary. You're always just the same." Holding the doll in her arms, Kathleen went to the window and stood looking out, feeling comforted by Adelaide Mary's silent, faithful presence.

The usual hour for breakfast came and Mrs. Webb called Kathleen, saying, "Ted and the girls will just have to eat whatever is left." Kathleen, still holding Adelaide Mary, followed Aunt Mel into the dining room. Mrs. Webb smiled as her daughter drew up an extra chair and carefully seated the doll.

"Why, this seems like old times, when Adelaide Mary was always with us," she said. "Since you began making rugs, Kathleen, you haven't had much time for Adelaide, have you?"

Kathleen shook her head. She was thinking that May Day was spoiled, that Ted and Janet and Beth had taken her very own pony and were probably having a fine time galloping about the fields, and none of them had wanted her. The choky feeling that Kathleen so dreaded prevented her from speaking aloud as she fought back tears. And when Aunty Mel said, "I don't see whatever possessed Ted to take the twins off at so early an hour," Kathleen gave her a loving look. Aunty Mel, she thought, was even a better friend than poor silent Adelaide Mary. After breakfast Kathleen kept very close to Aunt Mel as they all went out to the yard to look for Ted and the twins. But a full hour passed before Kathleen, standing near the lilac bushes with Adelaide Mary in her arms, saw a queer little parade coming along the road. Patch led the way, with Janet and Beth on his back. Beside them walked Ted, leading the brown pony, and Kathleen quickly noticed that Frisk limped. At this she completely forgot Adelaide Mary, letting the doll slip from her arms to the branches of a stout little bush,

51

where it lay staring up at its careless owner. But Kathleen was off like a flash, and as the tired and disappointed Ted, who was limping a little himself, started up the driveway, Kathleen was there to meet him. "What have you done to my pony, you hateful Ted Webb?"

Before Ted could respond, Beth came scrambling down from the back of the patient Patch, her round face tear-stained and bruised from a recent tumble, her dark curls tangled and untidy. Her voice came out broken and unhappy as she stammered, "It's my fault, Kathleen. Truly it is; I let Frisk out of the stable—"

Then, to Kathleen's amazement, Janet stepped forward, declaring, between sobs, that *she* was to blame. "I stole Ted's horse and then it ran away, and I fell off and hurt my wrist," she said.

By this time Aunt Mel had come outside to the group. She examined Janet's bruised hand and wrist a little anxiously and led her to the house, followed by Beth and Kathleen. Mr. Webb and Ted went to the stable, and Ted told his father the whole story of the morning's adventure: of Janet's being thrown from the back of Patch, of the discovery of Beth resting beside the road, and of finding the discouraged pony grazing in a nearby field. "Those girls might have been killed," Ted declared, as he told his father that Janet and Beth had each planned to "practice" riding horseback.

As Ted talked, Mr. Webb unstrapped the knapsack from the saddle. He now turned a questioning look toward his son, and Ted nodded as if in answer. "Yes, Father! I was off to join the army. I knew it was no use asking you again, and you know the army needs men. President Lincoln has asked for men." The fifteen-year-old boy straightened his shoulders, his face serious and anxious as if he alone were responsible for the success or failure of the Northern cause.

"Yes, Ted, I know," Mr. Webb responded gravely, and in the talk that followed there was no word of blame for Ted. Nevertheless, as they turned toward the house the boy firmly resolved that he would never again run away from home, and that when he joined the army, as he still intended to do, he would tell his father and mother of his intention.

"After all, Ted, it is lucky that Patch was saddled when Janet decided to ride horseback," said Mr. Webb. Ted answered quickly, "And that I was in time to find the girls, and Patch and Frisk, before more damage was done."

Ted ate a hearty breakfast, his mother filling his plate with crisp bacon and scrambled eggs as she listened to his story of the morning's adventures.

Hitty carried a tray up to the front bedroom where Janet, with her left hand neatly bandaged by Aunt Mel, sat at a small round table facing Beth, whose bruised cheek had been tenderly cared for. Both girls were wearing dresses of Kathleen's, as their own had been soiled and torn so badly that Aunt Mel knew they could not be worn again.

Hitty set the tray on the little round table. "I'll bring up some hot batter cakes and honey in just a minute," she announced, and trotted off. Kathleen served Janet and Beth some hot porridge and filled the pretty blue mugs with hot cocoa. "It's fun to have breakfast upstairs," she said happily. Janet and Beth both nodded. They had hardly spoken since confessing their blame in letting Patch and Frisk run off. They were both ashamed and sorry for the trouble they had caused by their thoughtlessness. Janet and Beth were sure that Kathleen must be angry with them. They were both a little homesick and had quite forgotten the beautiful muslin dresses, and even that it was May Day. Then, as they began eating the porridge, Kathleen suddenly darted from the room. Janet leaned across the table and whispered, "She's mad at us. She's run away!" and tears gathered in Beth's hazel eyes as she nodded in agreement and stammered, "O-oh, Janet, I—I wish we were home."

But before either of them could say anything more, Kathleen was back with a flower-filled basket in each hand. She smiled so radiantly that Janet and Beth found themselves smiling, too. When they discovered that the baskets had been made especially for them, and read the May Day verses, their troubles were forgotten and they once again felt like the happy young girls who had arrived at the farm.

"It's too late for our picnic, Aunty Mel says," said Kathleen, as Hitty appeared with hot cakes and honey, "and I guess you are both too tired, anyway."

Janet and Beth agreed that they were tired, and then Beth again became a little upset as she remembered they had spoiled the well-worn dresses that their mother had so carefully mended for this visit. Kathleen eyed Beth's serious face and said quickly, "Your mother will have to put tucks in those dresses, even if I have outgrown them. You see, being a year older makes a lot of difference," she explained. As the twins realized that the pretty dresses they were wearing were theirs to keep, Janet exclaimed, "Whatever makes you give us so many things?" Kathleen smiled with delight, for she was finding that it was a lot more fun to give presents than she had ever before realized. Ted walked by the open doorway and nodded approvingly as he noticed the girls' smiling faces. Suddenly Kathleen jumped up, exclaiming, "Oh, whatever has become of her!"

"If you mean Adelaide Mary, why I can tell you! I found her in the garden and she's downstairs," said Ted, going to his own room.

"I'll run down and get her," said Kathleen, and darted off.

"Who is Adelaide Mary?" asked Beth in a whisper. Janet shook her head. "Oh! I s'pose it's some other girl come to visit Kathleen." The twins were silent, for they felt disappointed that a strange girl was coming to share their visit.

In a moment they heard Kathleen's voice saying, "Yes, Adelaide Mary, I forgot all about you, poor dear, but I love you just the same," and the twins again had a twinge of homesickness, thinking that this Adelaide Mary must surely be Kathleen's dearest friend. A moment later, Kathleen appeared in the doorway, and in her arms was a big doll wearing a dress of green plaid silk.

"Let me introduce Adelaide Mary," said Kathleen.

CHAPTER 7

SELLING A RUG

IT WAS LATE IN the afternoon when Aunt Melvina and the Ross girls began their drive home. Kathleen stood at the gate, with Adelaide Mary in her arms, and sadly watched them leave. She was greatly disappointed that her mother had refused to allow her to return home with her aunt. Now, Kathleen told herself, the box with the two gold pieces would never be found. "I might just as well not look for it after such a long time," she thought, and decided to consult Hitty about possible purchasers of hooked rugs. For the moment Kathleen tried to comfort herself with the memory of the twins' delight in their white muslin dresses. They had started for home happy to own much better frocks than they had worn on their arrival at the Webb farm. Although she reminded herself that these dresses were worth as much as the lost money, Kathleen found little satisfaction in that fact, and as the days passed she became more and more

57

determined to earn enough to give the twins the money she had lost. Mrs. Webb was surprised to find that despite the pleasant spring weather, Kathleen seemed eager to sit inside the house at the rug frame drawing the bits of green wool through the loosely woven burlap. Hitty was sadly puzzled by Kathleen's constant questions about how to sell a rug; finally she concluded that Kathleen must want to sell the rug to earn money for a present for some member of the family. Hitty did her best to be of use, assuring Kathleen that it would be easy to find a customer who would gladly pay five dollars for a pine-tree rug.

As May of 1863 came to an end, the Union forces under General Hooker had suffered defeat at Chancellorsville, with great losses—thirty thousand men either wounded or dead. Now more than ever the Confederates felt invincible, and General Lee confidently expected that he could invade Northern territory, perhaps even win the war on Northern soil. Ted and his parents knew that every day brought this danger closer. Even Kathleen, absorbed as she was in her quest to restore the missing gold pieces and tell Aunty Mel the story of her "joke," understood that the situation was serious. She stopped repeating her wish that Lee would come to Gettysburg so that she could see him. For gradually the little girl was coming to realize that an invading army, no matter how impressive its commanding general may be, is something to be feared, and even as she questioned Hitty,

Kathleen recalled what her father had said to Ted that very morning. "You may be a soldier within a month, my boy; for if Lee's troops come this way we will all have to fight." Kathleen remembered Ted's somber face as he responded, "I'd do my best, sir." Now Kathleen, without waiting for Hitty's answer about a possible purchaser of the rug, suddenly exclaimed, "Oh, Hitty! Whatever will we do if war comes to Gettysburg?"

"My goodness. I suppose we wouldn't do anything. But what are you troubling about war for? I'm figuring out a way for you to sell that rug, and I've got it! Yes—I know just how it can be sold!" Hitty's face beamed with satisfaction as Kathleen eagerly demanded to hear the plan.

"Here's the way, Miss Kathleen. First of all you can tell your mother that you think you'll just ride your pony down the road, maybe as far as Mrs. McPherson's. That will be all right," Hitty nodded reassuringly. "And you can take along your rug and show it to Mrs. McPherson. When you point out to her how fine it is, she'll probably declare right away that she wants to buy it!" The triumphant Hitty drew a long breath of satisfaction as if Kathleen's rug had already found a buyer.

"Oh, Hitty! I do believe that is a good plan. I'll go tomorrow," said Kathleen, "and perhaps Mrs. McPherson may know of someone who will buy the other one."

"What other one?" asked Hitty.

"Why, the other one I am going to make! You see, Hitty, I must earn ten dollars, two five-dollar gold pieces," Kathleen explained.

"Well, then why don't you just ask ten dollars for *this* rug?" questioned Hitty hopefully, but Kathleen shook her head. It seemed doubtful to Kathleen that anyone would pay even five dollars, and she had already decided that even if she were offered only two dollars for the rug she must take it. "Then I'll have to make five rugs," she thought, "and that would take all summer." Nevertheless Kathleen was very hopeful that her pretty pine-tree rug would find a customer in Mrs. McPherson. "And if she doesn't want it, I know just what I'll do. I'll ride on and stop at each house until somebody does buy it," she decided. The next morning she asked her mother if she could ride Frisk over to the McPherson farm, several miles distant.

"Frisk isn't lame now, and Ted says I ought to ride him every day," she explained. Mrs. Webb agreed that if the next day were pleasant, Kathleen could ride over to see Mrs. McPherson.

"And you had best wear your new pink gingham dress," said Mrs. Webb.

"And my new hat?" asked Kathleen, for her new hat of white straw, with a big pink rose just under the left brim, seemed like exactly the right hat for the occasion. Her mother's smiling reply that "all new hats have to be worn the first time, don't they!" sent Kathleen racing upstairs to pull the hat from its box and lay it on the table where she would see it in the morning. As she held the pretty hat up to admire its beauty, Kathleen told herself that her mother was surely the best mother a little girl could have. "She's always so nice," Kathleen thought.

The next morning, the last day of May, was clear and pleasant. Hitty had carried the rug, carefully wrapped, to the stable and fastened the clumsy bundle to the front of Kathleen's saddle. Right after breakfast Kathleen said good-bye to her mother and, followed by Hitty, who insisted on seeing her off, ran into the yard. There stood Frisk, all saddled and ready to start.

"Now, Miss Kathy, don't you forget to smile when you offer that rug!" Hitty solemnly warned her as Kathleen, wearing the new pink gingham dress and the pretty hat, gathered up the reins and prepared to start. Kathleen nodded, and with a word to Frisk she rode down the driveway and onto the road leading to South Mountain. Frisk trotted along, nearly as happy as his young owner to be out on the smooth road in the fragrant air. Kathleen's copper-colored hair flew back from her face and her blue eyes were bright with pleasure. Perhaps before the end of another month she could give Aunty Mel a white box containing two five-dollar gold pieces, she thought hopefully. But beneath her happy thoughts was the wish that she had confessed to her aunt the moment she knew of the loss. That would have been so much easier.

That very morning, when Mrs. Webb had asked Kathleen what she meant to do with the rug, Kathleen had impulsively replied, "I am going to sell it and give the money to the Ross girls." Mrs. Webb said that would be a very good plan and thought proudly that her daughter was surely the most generous-hearted girl in the world. Kathleen couldn't wait to come trotting home from her ride with the price of the rug in her pocket.

Frisk was now climbing a steep hill. At the top he came to a standstill, looking over his shoulder as if to tell his rider that it was time for a fat pony to rest. Kathleen quite understood him and laughed delightedly as she dismounted and led him into the shade of a wide-spreading oak. From where she stood, Kathleen could see across the broad fields and slopes of cultivated farmlands to the ridges and mountains rising in the distance; in between there were deep forests, sheltering groves, and gently flowing streams. Turning toward the highway she could see the town of Gettysburg, nestled among fields and hills and sparkling in the May sunshine, with Oak Ridge rising beyond it: Oak Ridge, home of the seminary, where Kathleen was sure the missing box had been lost. As Kathleen gazed over valley and forest, she decided that it would be easy enough to ride

Frisk straight to Oak Ridge; either of the broad high-ways would lead to it.

"I'll go! It's only four miles!" she exclaimed. "I'll have plenty of time to ride Frisk over and get home before lunchtime, and maybe I can find the box. Oh, if I only could find it!"—and in another moment she had mounted the pony and was urging him over the road toward Oak Ridge at his best pace.

CHAPTER 8

THE WRONG ROAD

OAK RIDGE, WHICH only a few weeks later was to be renamed "Seminary" Ridge by the contending armies, is crossed by a number of roads. Kathleen was sure she could find her way without entering the town of Gettysburg or taking any chance of being seen by her Aunt Mel or any acquaintances.

"But if I do find the box, I'll take it straight to Aunty Mel; and if I don't find the box I'll sell this rug. I'll begin just as Hitty told me to, by asking Mrs. McPherson if she would like to see a pretty hooked rug that I have just made." Kathleen smiled happily thinking that this pleasant springtime road was sure to lead her to the end of all her worries about the lost box.

Now and then she looked over at the carefully rolled rug, and she had a fleeting wish that she had brought Adelaide Mary for company. Kathleen had so few playmates that her doll really was a special friend.

"But I guess carrying a doll wouldn't look very grown-up," she decided, not wanting to look too childish. Then her thoughts flew to the conversation at the breakfast table that morning. Her father had said that no one could say where the Confederates would enter Pennsylvania, and that there were rumors of Southern soldiers already on the march. He had added that probably their scouts were everywhere on the alert and had referred to the two whose conversation Kathleen had overheard at the ledge some weeks before.

As her pony trotted briskly over the smooth road, Kathleen felt proud that she had reported that conversation. The Union soldier said she had helped the Northern Army by warning of a possible invasion of Northern states. She recalled Ted's serious determination to become a soldier and wished there were some way in which a little Yankee girl could, if war really came near her home, be of use.

"But I do wish General Robert E. Lee was on our side," she thought, for she did greatly admire him.

Kathleen had been so intent on her thoughts, so pleased with the pony's even pace and the soft warm air, that she had not paid much attention to the direction. Now there was no familiar object in sight, but still she felt no uneasiness. She was sure the road would soon bring her in sight of Oak Ridge, for she did not know that Frisk had turned at a curve of the highway and was going directly away from the seminary.

Now and then some farmer would drive past Kathleen, waving a friendly greeting. Frisk trotted happily along until an old wagon, pulled by a tired gray horse and driven by a man in worn, shabby clothes, came to a halt right in the middle of the roadway. Frisk had to stop, too, but Kathleen was not at all frightened, for she supposed that the man had not seen her in time to move out of the way. She smiled a greeting, but the driver of the dilapidated wagon did not move or speak. Kathleen gazed at him in sudden alarm.

"I do believe he's asleep!" she exclaimed, and at that moment the man's eyes opened and he stared at Kathleen in surprise.

"What road is this?" he questioned sharply, straightening his shoulders briskly.

"I'm afraid I don't know, only that it goes near the seminary on Oak Ridge," Kathleen replied. At this the man's face became alert and he jumped quickly from his old wagon.

"Surely not! What a fool I am to get off my course like that," he muttered. Backing his tired horse, he turned his wagon around to face in the same direction as Kathleen. Then he gave another sharp look at the young girl in her pretty dress and hat riding the fat brown pony.

"Are you headed for the seminary, young lady?" he asked, and Kathleen replied with a smile, "Yes, sir." She would have moved on past the wagon but the man's hand grabbed Frisk's bridle rein, forcing her to ride alongside him.

"Not so fast. You surely want to help a traveler who has lost his way," he said, and Kathleen again replied, "Yes, sir! But I thought it likely you were a farmer, and perhaps knew the way better than I do. And I surely do not see Oak Ridge." Puzzled, she looked down the broad highway in the direction where she believed the seminary to be.

"I'll wager you don't know any better than I do," muttered the man, "even if you were born in Gettysburg."

"Oh, I wasn't born in Gettysburg. I was born in Maine," Kathleen promptly announced, and the man's dark eyes rested on her with even a sharper interest as he said, "A little Yankee girl, eh? And I suppose your father is a Yankee soldier." Without waiting for an answer, he asked sharply: "What are you going to the seminary for?"

"I lost a box there. I lost it a month ago—a little white box with two gold pieces in it!" Kathleen said. At the man's exclamation, she added, "And nobody knows it!"

"Then no one knows that you are going there this morning?" said the man thoughtfully.

"No, sir. I started out to sell my pine-tree rug; it's in this bundle." Kathleen touched the roll fastened to the front of her saddle. She did not feel at all afraid of this dark-eyed stranger with the pleasant voice, and she went on to tell him that Frisk had been a present on her eleventh birthday. The man smiled and said that he hoped his own little daughter might get a pony exactly like Frisk when she turned eleven. Kathleen began to feel that she had made a friend.

"Where is your little girl?" she asked, thinking how nice it would be if his little girl could come and visit her and learn to ride Frisk. But the man only shook his head and said, "Far away, little Yankee girl," in so sad a voice that for the first time Kathleen began to wonder about him.

"What is your little girl's name?" she asked.

At that moment Frisk swerved off the highway onto a narrow road. He was going so fast that Kathleen could scarcely control him, but she could hear the rattle of the wagon behind her and realized the stranger was following. The road grew suddenly narrow, and just ahead Kathleen could see a solidly built fence. The pony stopped short, apparently as surprised as Kathleen, and a moment later the stranger was standing beside Frisk, looking angrily at Kathleen.

"What sort of a trap is this you've led me into? Telling me you were on the right road to the seminary and I, fool enough to believe a Yankee, turning back on my course. We've been riding straight away from Gettysburg!" he said, and drew a worn silver watch from his pocket. "Look at the time! Twelve o'clock!"

"Oh, my goodness!" exclaimed Kathleen. "And it was not yet nine when I left home. I must indeed have taken the wrong road. My poor Frisk must be tired." Without a glance at the stranger, Kathleen slid from her saddle and began smoothing the pony's head and promising him a drink and something to eat. As the Confederate scout listened, he gave a quick breath of relief and his face softened, for he knew that this young girl had not purposely misled him, but had, as she said, lost her own way.

"I can hear the noise of a brook, and my poor horse will welcome a drink. I'll unhitch him and lead them both down to the creek," said the man, speaking again in a kindly tone. He led the two tired animals through the little grove toward Rock Creek, while Kathleen leaned against the stout fence and wondered where on earth her brown pony had brought her.

"I must start home as soon as Frisk is rested," she thought a little anxiously, knowing that even now her mother and Hitty would be expecting her return. Her thoughts were interrupted by the sound of breaking branches, and Frisk dashed through the underbrush as if pursued by some dangerous enemy. He came to a standstill with his nose against the gate close beside his small owner.

"Why, Frisk! Whatever is the matter?" asked the startled girl, looking around for some sign of danger. But the woods and fields seemed deserted; there was no sound other than the squawk of a distant blue jay and scolding chitter of a curious gray squirrel that was scooting along the top of the fence not far from the gate.

Kathleen, with her hand on the pony's bridle rein, stood looking anxiously toward the creek. Every moment she expected to hear steps and to see the shabby stranger and his gray horse appear from among the trees. But time passed, and except for Frisk's uneasy movements, nothing disturbed the quiet.

Kathleen was sure that her pony had not had his much needed drink, and she was now thirsty herself, as well as hungry. Thinking that the stranger must have ridden off, leaving his wagon, Kathleen decided to look for a place where she and Frisk could both drink. "And then we'll start back the way we came," she thought.

But before venturing into the underbrush, Kathleen took off her pretty hat and put it carefully on the seat of the old wagon. "I guess it will be safe there," she thought. Then she guided Frisk toward the slope that led, she was quite sure, to a stream. She had been wise to leave her hat on the wagon seat, she noted, for brambles and thorny branches caught at her dress and she had to be careful not to slip. Finally, pushing through a thick growth of bushes, with the pony resolutely pulling back, Kathleen exclaimed aloud, for she found herself almost at the edge of a steep rocky bank. Below her flowed the creek, and if Frisk had not held back so steadily, she might easily have plunged into the icy water. She had a glimpse of Oak Ridge in the distance, but had no time to look, for Frisk, now eager to reach the stream, was pulling strongly toward a rocky slope to their left. He now became the leader as Kathleen, clinging to his mane, stumbled on beside him until they reached the edge of the stream. There she slipped the bit from the pony's mouth so that he could drink in comfort. For herself, Kathleen made a clumsy cup from a broad oak leaf.

Once Frisk had waded eagerly into the water, Kathleen could see that it was going to be difficult to persuade him to come out. He ambled over to a grassy point that stretched into the stream and was about to settle down on his side when Kathleen's sharp call stopped him.

"Hold on, Frisk. I guess I'd better take off your saddle first," Kathleen said, reluctant to delay her start for home, yet sure that her pony could rest better if freed from his burden. She unstrapped the saddle and carried it a short way up the bank. Then she put the rug down beside it. Her pony was too tired to go any farther for the moment. He could feed on the young grass nearby.

"I'm tired myself," thought Kathleen, "and I do wish I had thought to take along some lunch." She had just sat down with her back leaning against the saddle when she heard a voice. It seemed to come from the foot of the rocky slope: "Hullo! Little Yankee girl! Little Yankee girl!" someone called.

CHAPTER 9

OVER THE CLIFF

KATHLEEN JUMPED UP with an exclamation of surprise and instantly called back, "I'm right here on the slope!" She looked eagerly in the direction of the voice, but there was no one to be seen.

"I'm hurt! Fell over the cliff" came the response, and in an instant Kathleen was running toward the foot of the wooded cliff over which she herself had so nearly tumbled.

Just as she reached the bottom, a number of good-sized rocks came tumbling through the bushes, almost crashing into her. The man called again, "I don't know if you can climb up here, and I don't know if you can help me. I reckon my ankle is broken, and beside that I'm wedged between rocks."

"I'm sure I can help you," Kathleen said eagerly. "I know I can climb up there. Anyway, I'm sure there's a farmhouse up beyond that house and I can run over there and get someone."

"No! No!" shouted the man. "Promise not to bring anyone here. Promise," he repeated, his voice shrill and anxious, so that the puzzled girl instantly answered, "I will do whatever you tell me!"

"That's better. Now try and come up toward the right of the scrub oak, and then you'll see me," he replied, "and maybe I can throw you down a package that I'll want you to carry to Gettysburg for me. But you must come carefully," he cautioned. Kathleen began to make her way among the rough underbrush and rocks at the base of the cliff, looking up at long stretches of smooth rock that made her realize how great a danger she had escaped when Frisk had pulled her back from the edge.

"I guess it's lucky the man got wedged in the rock after all," she thought as she scrambled up the face of a ledge. Some stout little spruce trees were rooted in the crevices, which gave her something to hold on to.

As she reached the top of this ledge the man called again, "Well done, little Yankee girl! I'm up here. Can you see me?" Looking up, Kathleen exclaimed in surprise and alarm, for the dark face of the stranger was peering over a high rock that seemed about to pitch over the face of the cliff.

As Kathleen stood staring up at her new acquaintance, she noticed more crevices along the ledge, and some small spruce trees here and there. She felt sure she could reach the spot where the man was imprisoned.

"I'm coming up. It's good climbing," she told him, and again the man cautioned her to be careful. Kathleen bravely began to make her way upward. Now and then her foot slipped and she had to grab hold of some pliant little sapling to keep from falling. Once or twice a loose rock gave way beneath her feet, and only her quickness saved her. Although it seemed like a long time, in only a few moments Kathleen found herself at the edge of the narrow crevice where the man had fallen. He was standing with his back against a wall of stone. His face was bruised and scratched.

As Kathleen appeared, he drew a long breath of relief and smiled broadly. Kathleen said, "Now I'll help you get down!"

"I begin to believe you will," declared the man, "but I don't know just how. Look!" and he nodded toward the left. Kathleen, stepping into the crevice, could see that his feet were both wedged firmly beneath a mass of rock.

"That rock came down with me," said the man, "and it would take a good while to dig it off my feet. I reckon my feet, from the way they feel, are pretty well smashed. I wish to goodness that I had never met up with you and your fat pony." A scowl crept over his dark face. If it were not for this girl, he would have completed his mission by now. For this shabby traveler was one of the many scouts sent out ahead of Lee's army to gather information about food and horses that the Confederates could secure near Gettysburg.

Lee's men were already moving north, and the scout knew that his own delay was a serious problem. He had scribbled a letter to his commanding officer giving information about supplies available near Harrisburg, the capital of Pennsylvania. Lee planned to capture this city. The Confederate scout decided to use Kathleen, the Yankee girl, as his messenger if he could not go on himself, for his feet were badly wounded. But Kathleen knew none of this as she struggled to help the stranger trapped on the ledge.

Kathleen's face flushed. She wanted to tell the man that he need not have followed the pony, but she was now eager to help him and said again, "I'm sure I can pull those rocks off."

"No! I tried it. They go crashing and rolling down the cliff, making enough noise to rouse a city!" declared the man. He added quickly, "I don't want anyone to think me fool enough to tumble over a cliff."

But Kathleen was already tugging and pulling at one of the big rocks so firmly wedged around the man's feet. In spite of his fear of the noise, the scout leaned forward and tried to help her. Once or twice she succeeded in raising it a little, but not enough for the man to free himself, and as the heavy stone settled back he groaned with pain. Kathleen looked up at him anxiously and said, "If I slip another rock under the next time we push it, maybe that will help." He did not reply, except to nod, and Kathleen began to fear that he was seriously hurt. She tugged at the rock with a new determination to set him free. As the rock moved, she succeeded in kicking a smaller stone under it so it could not fall back. Then, with a great effort, the imprisoned man and the young girl succeeded in moving the rock enough for him to free his feet. As he did so, he sank back with a moan of pain and Kathleen realized that his feet were badly hurt and he could not stand. For a moment she hardly knew what to do other than break her promise and hurry off to bring help. But the man drew himself into a sitting position and began to pull off his heavy, clumsy shoes. These had protected his feet somewhat, but he was clearly in pain.

"I'd give anything for a bucket of cold water," he said, as if speaking to himself, and Kathleen remembered the tin bucket that hung from the back of his rickety wagon. "I'll bring it!" she declared. "I can climb up from here and get the bucket and bring some water."

"You're a good soldier!" said the man, looking gratefully at the child who seemed now to think only of helping this unknown stranger. "I reckon I'll have to let you try," he added thoughtfully, as if he were sorry to trouble her.

"There's a box of food in that wagon," he continued. "I reckon we could both do with a bite. And there's a blanket." Although he did not suggest that Kathleen attempt to bring these things, she instantly decided to make as many trips to the wagon as was needed to get them. Then she started off to discover an easy path up the cliff.

Turning to the right, she followed the ledge until it gradually grew less steep. The path was rough, but she climbed steadily on. Just before reaching the wooded top she heard a bubbling sound and looked about anxiously. "That sounds like a brook," she thought. But it was not a brook; it was a spring of clear water that came bubbling up at the foot of a ledge just above where Kathleen was standing.

"It looks just like our spring!" she exclaimed, and for a moment a sense of fear and homesickness tempted Kathleen to forget her promise to the injured stranger. She could find some farmhouse where help would be sent to him and then go straight to her home.

But it was only for a moment, for Kathleen remembered the man's words, "You're a good soldier." The thought, too, of the stranger's own little girl, who was far away, made Kathleen decide not to desert him but to do her best to help him. After a drink of the cool water she hurried over the short distance to the deserted road and the old wagon.

After unfastening the bucket, Kathleen pulled a box from under the wagon seat, and found a rolled up blanket. The box fit into the bucket, and she was sure she could carry both blanket and pail down to the crevice in the cliff.

Then she turned to look at her pretty hat resting on the worn leather cushion of the wagon seat. "I guess I'll put it under the seat," she decided, and she spread a handful of tall grass on the dusty bottom of the old wagon and put her hat under the shelter of the seat. Then taking up bucket and blanket she started back.

At the spring she left the blanket and the box of food. "I guess I can manage to carry the pail half-full," she thought, and in spite of the rough way Kathleen succeeded in reaching the crevice with the pail half-filled with spring water.

The man drank thirstily and then began to bathe his swollen feet and ankles with the cool water.

"If I only had something to bandage them with," he muttered.

"Would the ruffle on my dress do?" asked Kathleen. She looked regretfully at her new pink gingham dress—the dress that only that morning had been so fresh and pretty but now was soiled and torn.

"Indeed it would. I'll cut the stitches with my knife, and you shall never regret it," said the man as he pulled out a pocketknife and with careful hands ripped off the wide ruffle. Kathleen helped him fasten the wet bandages around his ankles, and when this was done she sped back to the spring for the food and blanket.

"It's too warm for a blanket, but maybe it will be good for your feet," she said. Almost too tired to take another step, Kathleen sank down on a moss-covered rock at the entrance of the crevice.

The man opened the box and held it out to Kathleen.

"Thank you. I am dreadful hungry," she said, so seriously that the man smiled and told her to help herself. Kathleen took a square of hard gingerbread from the box, a slice of chicken, and a biscuit, then handed the box back to her companion. "Have you seen my gray horse?" he asked.

Kathleen shook her head. She had entirely forgotten about the gray horse, and the man said it had probably made its way into some nearby field.

"I'd find Old Ned quickly enough if I could walk," he said.

"My pony is down by the creek," said Kathleen, and her companion nodded thoughtfully.

"You must rest an hour, and then lead your pony back to the road and start back to Gettysburg. I want you to take a letter for me," he continued, "and you must tell me your name and where your home is."

"How will you get along without me?" asked Kathleen, but her face brightened as she realized that very soon she would be on Frisk's back heading toward home.

"I'll manage. I'll crawl to the spring. Then I'll be all right," he said. An hour later, with Kathleen tugging the bucket and blanket, he did indeed crawl within reach of the bubbling water, where he sank down exhausted.

"Now, little Yankee girl, here is a letter that must reach the Gettysburg post office tonight."

Kathleen took the white envelope that the man drew from his pocket, and said, "I'll try not to lose it."

"You *mustn't* lose it," he warned her. "You have a pocket, haven't you?"

Kathleen nodded. "Yes, a deep pocket!" she replied. The man handed her the letter, which she put carefully into her pocket.

"Now here is something you are not to look at until you get home," he said, giving Kathleen a small firm package. "It's a present," he added, noticing her wondering look.

"Thank you. I won't look at it until I get home," said Kathleen, smiling as she thought of how surprised her mother would be to hear of the day's adventure.

"Now be off. You brought me into this trouble, but you have proved yourself a friend and a soldier," said the man, and his thin brown fingers clasped Kathleen's hand as he bade her good-bye.

"Please give my love to your little girl," Kathleen called over her shoulder as she started toward the creek.

"Indeed I will, little Yankee girl," the man responded, adding to himself, "If I ever see my little girl again," for he knew well what lay before him—dangers not only in his work as a scout for the Confederate Army, but the dangers of the great battle between the Northern and Southern armies that was drawing nearer every day.

"HERE IS A LETTER THAT MUST REACH THE GETTYSBURG
POST OFFICE TONIGHT"

CHAPTER 10

"BUTTONS"

FRISK WAS EASILY caught, and Kathleen led him as near as possible to where she had left her saddle and the rug. As she looked at the rug the little girl impulsively decided to climb up to the spring and give the rug to the man who, she felt sure, was stuck there for the coming night.

"It will be something like a bed, anyway," thought Kathleen, for the moment forgetting her debt to the little Ross girls, as well as her plan to sell the rug, and thinking only of the look of pain on the stranger's face. After all, it was her pony Frisk's dash from the highway that had led the traveler to his tumble over the cliff.

"And he gave me a present," she reflected. "Maybe it's soldiers' buttons!" At this thought a little smile crept over her face, for in 1863, every little Yankee child was eager to possess some of the shin-

85

ing brass buttons with the raised, winged eagle that were used on the soldiers' coats.

Fastening Frisk's bridle rein to a stout sapling, Kathleen picked up the closely rolled rug and started back up the slope to the spring. This was a much easier climb than the one she had made up to the rocky crevice, and she soon approached the bubbling waters of the spring. "I'm bringing you something," she called and then rounded the ledge to the spot where she had left the traveler.

"Oh! He's gone!" she exclaimed, looking around and seeing no trace of the man. The blanket and box of food had vanished as well. There was nothing to show that an hour earlier the spring had been the center of an encampment. But Kathleen's disappointment vanished instantly as she heard the stranger's voice. "You gave me a nice fright!" he called. "What brought you back?" She turned and saw his head rising above a growth of tall bushes where he had concealed himself.

"Oh! I didn't think you'd be afraid!" she exclaimed. "I only came to bring you a rug. It's mine. I can do what I like with it, and I want to give it to you," and she hurriedly began to unroll the bundle. "Here it is! A pine-tree rug, to remember me by." She ran toward the bushes to give it to her new friend, and as he reached up to take the rug Kathleen saw tears on his thin cheeks. For a moment she felt ready to cry herself. But the stranger's face brightened as he took the rug.

"Bless you, child. Now be off, and forget you ever saw me. Or, rather, forget to tell of seeing me. Will you do that?" he asked.

"Not tell anyone?" she questioned. "Why not?"

"Never mind why not. But do not speak of me to a living mortal. If you do, I'll never see my own little girl again!" he said.

"Oh, I won't tell. Truly I won't," Kathleen promised, "and you tell your little girl that I made the rug and drew the pattern!"

The man nodded, as if he were almost too weary to speak, and then said: "Thank you, child. I will remember your name, and some day you shall know mine, and maybe I can be of some service to you. Now start for home, and heaven guard you." Once more his thin brown fingers clasped the little girl's hand, and again he whispered: "Be off. Lose no time. Mail my letter." Then he sank back out of sight, and Kathleen hurried down the slope wondering why the man was so fearful of discovery. She felt vaguely uneasy about him, though she didn't know why.

Frisk started along the side of the hill and made his way back to the old wagon. Pressing his nose against the stout gate, he whinnied as if demanding that it be instantly opened. Kathleen rescued her treasured hat, and turned Frisk toward the highway. She urged him on until Frisk realized that he was now headed toward his new home. Once on the turnpike he trotted off so briskly that it was not long before

Kathleen began to see the familiar Oak Ridge and seminary building, and the familiar buildings of the town of Gettysburg. She remembered the letter, safe in the deep pocket of her gingham skirt, and told herself that she must ask the first person she met the way to the post office. Kathleen never even imagined that she was carrying a message for one of the scouts of Lee's army, a letter directed to a trusty sympathizer of the Confederate cause, with valuable information that would be promptly forwarded to Culpeper Court House, near Lee's cavalry headquarters.

The June afternoon was drawing toward sunset when Kathleen dropped the letter into the box at Gettysburg post office. Now she was free to turn Frisk onto the familiar road that would take her straight home. She no longer thought of trying to visit Oak Ridge, or of searching for the lost box; she was so tired that all she could think of was getting home. The many adventures of her long day already seemed far off in the past as Frisk turned into the driveway and Ted came out to take the pony by the bridle.

"Well, you have made a day of it, Katydid!" he said as he lifted her from the saddle. "Whatever has happened to your dress and shoes?" With his arm around his little sister, Ted looked with surprise at her torn and untidy dress and her muddy shoes. "Your hat seems all right, though," he added. Kathleen, leaning against him, said, "I took it off," but in so faint a voice that Ted was instantly sure some accident had befallen her. "Hitty! Hitty! come here!" he called, and Hitty came running from the kitchen with so frightened an expression that, tired though she was, Kathleen giggled in amusement.

"Oh, it isn't the Confederate Army, Hitty," said Ted. "It's only Katydid tired to death, and I reckon she fell off Frisk into a mud hole. You'd better take her in."

Kathleen was too tired to explain that she had not tumbled from the pony. She was glad to have the stout Hitty pick her up and carry her upstairs to her own pleasant room. And although Hitty exclaimed over the ruin of the pink gingham dress, asked reproachfully, "Where in the world is that grand ruffle?" and held up the shoes, scuffed and ruined by Kathleen's scramble at Rocky Creek, the girl said not a word of her tremendous adventure. Not until Hitty had helped her Kathleen into a pretty blue striped dress, fresh stockings and slippers, and was brushing her copper-colored hair, did the tired girl speak.

"Hitty, I gave the rug away!" she announced.

"My word, missy. Whatever for?" and the amazed and disapproving Hitty stood with uplifted hands. "And didn't you tell Mrs. McPherson that you wanted money for it?" she asked.

Kathleen slowly shook her head.

"I haven't been near the McPhersons'. Frisk took a wrong road, and he didn't want to come home, and—oh, everything, Hitty," Kathleen suddenly concluded, remembering that she was very nearly breaking her promise to the stranger whom, helpless and suffering, she had left on the steep slope of Rocky Creek.

"Who *did* you give that rug to?" demanded Hitty.

"To a friend of mine," Kathleen responded, and Hitty asked no more questions.

If Kathleen wished to give the rug to a friend, Hitty was sure that was far better than selling it to a stranger. The loyal Hitty even explained to Mrs. Webb that the reason Miss Kathleen was so late in returning home was that the pony had taken the wrong road, and when Kathleen sat down for the belated supper she looked so tired that her mother postponed questioning her. Besides, Ted had so much to tell of the recent news of the movements of Lee's Army of Northern Virginia, whose cavalry, in a single division, was under the command of General J. E. B. Stuart, that no one gave Kathleen any special notice.

It was the third day of June, 1863, and the news that Lee was concentrating his army at Culpeper had already reached Pennsylvania. Ted now eagerly reminded his father of the May Day promise that he could join the Union forces if the Confederates marched into Pennsylvania.

"Wait, my boy. Lee has not yet crossed the Potomac River. When he moves his men toward the Susquehanna then we will discover if he means to attack Harrisburg, and then we'll all have to do our best to defend our homes. Governor Curtin will call for men when the Keystone State needs them." Ted was forced to be satisfied with this, although he declared that Lee's scouts were everywhere.

"Why, Father, they travel about Pennsylvania as if they owned it! Sometimes they pretend to be farmers going to town with a wagonload of produce, and question everyone they meet. I'll wager they know just where to gather supplies for Lee's troops," said Ted. Mr. Webb agreed, but added that he believed General Hooker, commanding the Union troops stationed on the Rappahannock, was well aware of Lee's movements, and that Union scouts were as active as those of the Confederates.

When Ted spoke of scouts traveling about as farmers, Kathleen looked up quickly. It flashed through her thoughts that the traveler with her pine-tree rug might be one of those scouts Ted spoke of. Then, for the first time since reaching home, she remembered the little flat package in the pocket of her gingham dress—the brass buttons, she hoped and believed, of a Union soldier. And at the thought of the buttons, her fear that her new friend might be a Confederate scout vanished. She hurried through her supper and ran upstairs to find the gingham dress and examine the little package. The dress was not in her room; nor was it in the closet, and Hitty was again startled and amazed when Kathleen came rushing into her kitchen demanding, "Where *is* my pink

gingham dress, Hitty Marjorum? What did you do
with it?"

"My goodness! I didn't do anything with it,"
replied Hitty, rolling her eyes in annoyance at the
excited girl, and adding quickly, "And you aren't
paying any attention here at all, missy! Don't you see
this waffle iron waiting? Your father wants his waffles this instant!" Hitty turned back to the stove as if
a gingham dress was of no importance in comparison
with Mr. Webb's need of hot waffles.

But Kathleen was not so easily put off. Seizing
Hitty's arm, she again demanded, "What ever did
you do with my pink gingham dress?"

"What I did with that ruined dress was to throw it
right into the tub and pour water on it. That's all,
until I get the chance to scrub it out."

Kathleen hardly waited for Hitty to finish before
she dashed out of the kitchen into the adjoining shed
where the washtubs stood, and where the limp, soak-
ing gingham was quickly discovered in a well-filled
tub. With a little moan of disappointment, Kathleen
dragged the dress to the surface and turned the
pocket inside out, but the little package was gone!
Kathleen's first thought was that Hitty must have
taken it out; perhaps at this moment it was safe and
sound on the table in her room. But another possibility occurred to the little girl: the package might have
slipped from the pocket of the dress and now be at
the bottom of the washtub. Kathleen grasped the side

of the wooden tub, planning to tilt it so she could see if there was anything to be found. She pulled a bit too vigorously, and an instant later the tub slipped from its bench and toppled toward Kathleen, drenching her with water. As she jumped backward, the lurching tub knocked her over and nearly landed right on top of her.

Kathleen's shrieks brought Hitty and the entire family running to the shed, but before they reached her the little girl had seen two shining golden objects drop from the tub. She just managed to capture them.

CHAPTER 11

A DAY AT HOME

TED WAS THE FIRST one to reach the shed, and as he saw Kathleen floundering in the sweep of water from the overturned tub he exclaimed, "Well! Katy-*did* it this time!" He lifted his sister to her feet, holding her at arm's length so that her dripping garments would not touch him, and he laughed heartily at her pitiful appearance. Mrs. Webb was too anxious to get her daughter into dry garments to ask any questions. She hurried Kathleen into the house while Hitty, talking to herself and exclaiming over the flooded floor of the shed, lifted the tub back to its place.

"I didn't mean to upset it," whimpered Kathleen. "I wanted to find my pocket." She tightly clutched the shining objects she had rescued, and as she followed her mother into her own room she slipped them into a small box on the table. Mrs. Webb turned at that very moment and said, "Kathleen! Don't touch anything until you take off those wet clothes. And I think bed is

the best place for you the minute you are ready for it."
To her surprise, Kathleen promptly agreed.

"I'm so tired!" she declared as her head touched
the pillow. "I had to walk and walk," she added sleep-
ily, and almost before her mother left the room Kathleen was fast asleep.

When she awoke the next morning, the June sunlight filled her room with flickering gleams, and a
sparrow was singing about how pleasant it was to
balance on the branch of an oak tree with honeysuckle and jasmine in blossom nearby. Kathleen's
room was filled with the fragrance of early summer,
and for a few moments the young girl, half awake,
wondered if yesterday and all its adventures had
been only a dream. Then the memory of those queer
buttons that the stranger had given her made her
spring out of bed and across the room, eager to make
sure that the shining circles were really safe in her
small table.

Pulling out the drawer, Kathleen could hardly
believe that what she saw was real: for there, shining
up at her, were two gold pieces.

"O-ooh!" she whispered to herself. "Not buttons
at all!" and she picked up one of the gold pieces as
carefully as if she expected it to instantly turn into a
brass button.

"Each one is five dollars!" she said and her first
thought was that the stranger had made a mistake.
"He couldn't have meant to give me so much!" she

told herself. Then she quickly remembered that perhaps the man, even if he did have a little girl of his
own, might not know how much a Yankee girl would
value the brass buttons of a Union soldier.

"Maybe he thought five-dollar gold pieces were
better for a real present, and maybe he didn't have
any soldier buttons to spare," she decided thoughtfully.

"I'm glad I gave him my rug," she said to herself.
Recalling the rug, Kathleen's face brightened and
she began to feel as happy as the joyful sparrow. "It's
just like a true fairy story," she whispered, "and now
I can wrap these gold pieces up in a box just as Aunty
Mel did for Janet and Beth, and I can put the box
where one of them will find it! Oh, goody, goody!
Oh, it's splendid." Kathleen went hopping about the
room in her bare feet, feeling that all her worries
were over.

"I'll ask Mother to let me visit Aunty Mel right
away," she decided as she heard Hitty coming along
the hallway with the daily pitcher full of hot water for
the Kathleen's morning bath. She slipped the gold
pieces back into the drawer of the table and was eager
to get ready for breakfast. A little later, when Mrs.
Webb came into the room, she found her daughter
wearing a pretty gingham dress and ready to go downstairs. Mrs. Webb smiled as Kathleen exclaimed,
"Mother! I feel just the way that bird sounds!" for the
sparrow, swinging on another branch of the tall oak

tree, was again singing joyfully. "I could sing all morning in the sunshine."

"That's the way I want you to feel always," Mrs. Webb said, and she clasped Kathleen's hand in her own as they left the room. "Now tell me all about what happened yesterday!" she added.

Kathleen stopped suddenly and her happy face clouded. She remembered that she could not tell, not even her mother, about the stranger who had a little girl, and who had fallen over the cliff at Rocky Creek.

"Oh, Mother!" she exclaimed in so woeful a tone that Mrs. Webb looked at her little daughter in surprise at the sudden change. But thinking only that Kathleen did not want to recall a clumsy fall from Frisk's broad back, she did not question her daughter, except to say, "Well, dear, never mind. Only tell me what you did with your rug." Again Kathleen's half-whispered exclamation made her mother wonder if her daughter was not more tired out by her long day's absence from home than she had realized. As they reached the dining room she said gently, "You can tell me about it whenever you want to, dear child. As long as you got home safely, it's all right."

"And you don't feel too sorry about my tearing the ruffle from my new dress, and scuffing my shoes?" Kathleen asked. "Because, truly, I couldn't help it." Her blue eyes were so earnest and pleading as she looked up into her mother's face that Mrs. Webb quickly assured her that to have her safe and happy was far more important than any dress or shoes could possibly be. Hearing this, Kathleen's happy smile returned and she did not even mind Ted's teasing her about upsetting the tub. Before breakfast was over her father and mother had promised that she could visit her Aunt Melvina the coming week.

"And I may take Frisk?" she asked. "May I? Because I want Janet and Beth to ride him, and to help me teach him tricks, like bowing and shaking hands." And, although the disapproving Hitty, standing near the door leading to the kitchen, shook her head as if to warn the entire family of the dangers of such "doings," Mr. and Mrs. Webb agreed that Frisk could accompany Kathleen on her visit. Now Kathleen felt that all her problems were disappearing: she could replace the lost gift for the Ross girls, and her mother had said that she could tell of her yesterday's adventures when she was ready to, and not before.

Kathleen promised herself, however, to tell Aunty Mel about the "joke" she had planned—that she had lost the box containing the present for the twins and had then been afraid to tell of it.

"I will surely tell her just as soon as she knows that Janet and Beth have the money," she thought. "Maybe they'll think it wasn't really lost, after all."

With Adelaide Mary for company, Kathleen spent the morning in the house and garden. She had discovered a small box similar to the one that she had taken from Aunt Mel's dining room. Kathléen put the gold pieces into this box, wrapped it in white paper, and tied it securely. Then she began to think about a hiding place where it would not be discovered. A glance at her beloved Adelaide Mary solved this problem. "I'll make a deep pocket in your skirt, dear Adelaide Mary," she confided to her silent friend. Mrs. Webb, seeing her daughter happy and busy with her big doll, returned to her work in an upper room. She was preparing bandages and lint for use in the field hospitals of the Union Army.

Every day brought fresh news about the advance of Lee's army into Northern territory. Southern resources were giving out, and the Southern soldiers, although paying with Confederate notes for food, horses, and whatever they took, were determined to capture all provisions possible from the well-to-do people and fertile farms of the rich district toward which their troops were now headed.

As Mrs. Webb worked, she thought about the brave and loyal women of the South who, as faithful to the Confederate as she herself was to the Union cause, were working under great difficulties. She could hear Kathleen singing or talking to the faithful Adelaide Mary, and Mrs. Webb sent a friendly thought to the little girls of the neighboring states, and wished with all her heart that the great nation might once more be at peace.

Sitting there in her quiet room, Mrs. Webb knew that a tremendous battle, a battle that would mark the height of the Civil War, was near; and she feared, as did all the people along the Pennsylvania frontier, that it might come very near her own home. But Kathleen, looking forward to the delight of visiting Aunty Mel, with Adelaide Mary accompanying her, was troubled only when she recalled the stranger helpless and alone on the slope above Rocky Creek. Then, remembering that he had been able to drag himself along the rough hillside, and that he had said in another day he would be off, Kathleen's thoughts returned to Janet and Beth. Wouldn't they be just thrilled to discover the mysterious box with a five-dollar gold piece for each of them!

The sound of horse's hoofs on the driveway made Kathleen look up quickly from her work of stitching a pocket into Adelaide Mary's silken skirt. She caught a glimpse of Ted, mounted on Patch, as he turned onto the highway and galloped off toward Gettysburg. At that moment Hitty came over to the garden bench where Kathleen was seated.

"I've brought you a little plate of fresh-baked cookies, Miss Kathy!" she announced, handing Kathleen a plateful of plump sugar cookies still warm from the oven.

"Where has Ted gone?" Kathleen asked, after politely offering Adelaide Mary a cookie, which was silently refused.

"Well, Miss Kathy, so far as I can discover, your brother Ted has gone to join the war!" replied Hitty, her face becoming very grave as she continued: "Leastways, I heard Mr. Webb say something like that."

"Oh, Hitty! Ted can't go. He isn't old enough!" cried Kathleen, jumping up from the bench and quite forgetting both Adelaide Mary and the plateful of cookies at the thought of Ted amid the perils of war. Without waiting to ask any more questions, she ran to the house to ask her mother if Ted and Patch were really off to join the Army of the Potomac.

CHAPTER 12

TROUBLE

HITTY'S ANNOUNCEMENT that Ted had gone to join the war was quickly explained to Kathleen, who raced up the stairs calling, "Mother! Mother! Has Ted gone to be a soldier?"

"He has gone to Gettysburg to train for service with the boys at Pennsylvania College," replied Mrs. Webb, smiling at Kathleen's anxious expression. "And he will not be home again until we have news of the movements of the Union forces. Of course Ted is too young to be a soldier, but this training makes him happier. However, I hope it will soon be over." Mrs. Webb's face grew serious and her smile vanished. Mr. and Mrs. Webb, in giving their permission for Ted to train with the college boys, could not realize that within a month fifty-seven students from Pennsylvania College, together with four from the seminary and twenty-two other youths of the town, would be members of an "emergency infantry," in Company A,

Pennsylvania, and would be fighting very near their own homes. Ted, young as he was, would prove himself a worthy soldier.

"He didn't tell me good-bye," complained Kathleen, and then, thinking about her upcoming visit with Aunt Mel, she added quickly, "Perhaps I'll see him when I am at Aunty Mel's."

"Why, I would not be surprised," agreed Mrs. Webb. Reassured, Kathleen remembered the deserted cookies on the garden bench and fled back to pick up her big doll, making sure the little white box was safe in Adelaide Mary's pocket. Then she sat down contentedly to enjoy Hitty's delicious cookies.

The Webb farm lay on a pleasant slope, and from the garden bench Kathleen could look off to the distant heights of Blue Ridge Mountains. Toward the east rose Cemetery Ridge, and nearer at hand a wooded hill towered above the surrounding country. Looking at this hill Kathleen wondered why it had no name. From its northern side a bold shoulder stood out, the "Little Round Top," where in the battle of Gettysburg, Brigadier-General Weed was to die in its defense.

But there was no thought of battles in Kathleen's mind that June morning as she sat in the garden eating sugar cookies and looking out over the countryside. She was too busy planning all the good times that she would soon enjoy with Janet and Beth Ross, and she was eager to tell Aunt Mel the story of the lost box. In spite of all these pleasant possibilities, there was, however, a little shadowy worry in Kathleen's thoughts when she remembered that her adventure at Rocky Creek was a secret. She wanted to tell her mother and father all about it: to repeat what the stranger had said of her courage, of his own little girl, and to show them the gold pieces.

Kathleen sighed as she whispered to herself, "Maybe I can't ever tell them. Not unless the stranger comes to see us and says that I may. Perhaps he will come!" At this thought her face brightened. Anyway, she reflected, Janet and Beth would have the gold pieces. Just then two wide-winged gold and bronze butterflies fluttered over the bushes and a bright-breasted cardinal chirped, "Pret-*tee!* pretty! pretty!" Kathleen's shadowy troubles disappeared, and she and Adelaide Mary headed inside to Hitty's kitchen for a fresh supply of cookies and a glass of cool milk.

When the day came for Kathleen's visit to Aunty Mel's, the weather was perfect for riding Frisk to Gettysburg. Wearing her riding dress of blue linen and sailor hat of blue straw, Kathleen carried Adelaide Mary out to the yard. Frisk awaited them, all saddled and bridled.

Mr. and Mrs. Webb were accompanying their daughter. They sat in the comfortable Concord wagon drawn by one of the fine farm horses. Kathleen's small square trunk lay in the back of the wagon. Kathleen mounted her pony and kept pace beside the wagon, smiling with pleasure. Here she was, mounted on Frisk and bound for her aunt's with Adelaide Mary securely seated just in front of her. The little box for the Ross girls was safely hidden in the doll's pocket.

It seemed to Kathleen that the fields and hills had never been as beautiful as this June morning. The wide spreading field of wheat, the blues of the distant mountains, and the fragrance of many blossoms made it a scene of peace and beauty; Kathleen rode along gaily, unaware that marching armies were moving along highways and mountain passes toward these wooded slopes and open fields. For the Confederate and Union soldiers were soon to meet in a historic battle.

Aunt Melvina welcomed her guests warmly. She was always delighted to have her niece visit her, and now insisted that Kathleen stay until after July Fourth.

"All right," said Mrs. Webb. "But Kathleen must promise not to start out alone with Frisk," she added, telling of Kathleen's all-day absence from home. Aunt Mel and her niece both assured Mrs. Webb that Kathleen would not go out on Frisk without a companion.

"General Hooker is moving the Union Army northward to guard Washington," Kathleen heard her father say, and her Aunt Mel quickly responded, "And Lee knows that, for his scouts are everywhere. It is said one of them fell over a bluff at Rocky Creek last week, but managed to get off. He took two fine horses from a farm nearby, but he left a roll of Confederate money to pay for them."

"O-ooh!" whispered Kathleen, who was instantly sure that this Confederate scout must be the stranger to whom she had given her pine-tree rug, and whose gold pieces were at that very moment safe in the pocket of Adelaide Mary's silken skirt. Kathleen suddenly recalled how many questions the stranger had asked her, and her face flushed as she realized that she had told the man about her father's four horses, and that many of the neighboring farmers had fine young horses and many cattle. Kathleen began to feel herself almost a traitor to the cause of the Union, for which Ted was so eager to fight.

"There are rumors" said her father, "that this scout must have had friends in Gettysburg, who probably told him just where to look for good horses and fat cattle." At this Kathleen sobbed aloud.

"Why, Kathleen! Whatever is the matter?" exclaimed her mother, putting her arm about the unhappy child, while Aunt Mel looked at her niece in surprise.

"I believe I frightened the child with all this talk of scouts and battles," declared Mr. Webb, "but we must face the fact that both Northern and Southern armies are marching in this direction, and that before many weeks they will meet in battle."

But this was small comfort to Kathleen. "Oh, dear! Oh, dear!" she continued to sob, all her happy plans quite forgotten until Aunt Mel exclaimed, "Here come Janet and Beth!" At this Kathleen choked back her sobs, hastily wiped away her tears, and was able to smile a greeting to the delighted twins. They at once began to ask about Frisk and Patch, and exclaimed over Adelaide Mary, still held close in Kathleen's arms.

"May I take her?" asked Beth, reaching out her arms, quite sure that Kathleen would share her doll. But Kathleen drew back quickly, taking a firmer hold than ever on Adelaide Mary, for she was afraid Beth might discover the package hidden in the doll's pocket.

"Don't touch her!" she exclaimed in so sharp a voice that Beth and Janet both stared at her in amazement, for the twins had never before known Kathleen to be anything but friendly and unselfish. Beth's round face grew serious, and Janet clasped her sister's plump little hand and whispered, "Never mind, Beth; it's Kathleen's doll."

"Of course it's my doll," exclaimed Kathleen, "and when I want you to play with her, I'll tell you!" Hardly realizing what she said or did, the unhappy Kathleen turned and ran out of the room, leaving her astonished friends staring after her. Hand in hand, the twins stood near the door to Aunt Melvina's garden, where Mr. and Mrs. Webb and Aunt Melvina were deep in conversation.

"Maybe we'd better go home," said Janet. Beth nodded silently, and the two girls started down the garden path. Aunt Melvina ran after them.

"Wherever are you going, girls? And where is Kathleen? Didn't you understand that I invited you for dinner?" she questioned as she smiled at the sad faces of her little neighbors.

"Thank you very much, Miss Mel, but we must go home," Janet managed to say.

"Oh! that's too bad. Poor Kathleen will be disappointed. She brought her special doll and was planning a fine time with you this afternoon," said Aunt Melvina, and then her face grew serious, for poor little Beth, at the mention of Kathleen's doll, had begun to sniff, and tears were now rolling down her round cheeks.

"Why, Beth, dear!" Instantly Aunt Melvina's arms were around the little girl. "Do tell me what the matter is."

"Kathleen doesn't like us any more. She don't want us!" sobbed Beth.

CHAPTER 13

KATHLEEN DISAPPEARS

KATHLEEN FLED THROUGH the house to the backyard, raced across to the stables, and, hardly noticing her pony's welcoming whinny, stood for a moment looking around the big cool barn. The doors, open on each end, gave a view of Gettysburg on one side and of Seminary Ridge on the other. As she looked at the cupola of the seminary building, she recalled telling the stranger that from this cupola one could see South Mountain and many of the roads leading from Gettysburg to the west, southwest, and northwest. Remembering Aunt Mel's comment that the Confederate scouts were seeking not only supplies for Lee's army but a gathering place for his scattered troops, Kathleen again realized that she had told a Confederate scout the very best place in Gettysburg to watch for the advance of the Union forces.

"Oh, dear!" she whispered. "What can I do? I wish the Union Army would come first. I wish I could do

something to help President Lincoln. I wish—" but
the sound of voices made Kathleen look about a little
fearfully, for she was too upset to want anyone to find
her just then. Noticing a ladder against a hayloft, she
hurriedly scrambled up and concealed herself in the
heaped up hay. She had hardly settled herself before
two men entered the barn and, without a suspicion
that their conversation could be overheard, began to
talk excitedly.

"I tell you Lee's army is already in Pennsylvania,"
said one. "And I'll wager someone in our very town
helped that scout get away from Rocky Creek." Hearing this Kathleen held her hand firmly across her
mouth, fearful that she might call out that she had not
known the friendly stranger was an enemy to the
Union.

"Well," said another voice, "I'm off within an
hour to Harrisburg to join the militia, or I'd take my
chances on trying to reach General Hooker and let
him know that Lee's men are on the march toward
Chambersburg."

"Where would you find Hooker?" questioned the
first speaker scornfully. Kathleen forgot her fear of
discovery and leaned so far forward to hear the man's
reply that a bunch of loose hay tumbled from the loft.
The surprised men looked up to see a young girl,
holding a big doll, peering with startled eyes over the
edge of the hayloft!

"Great Scott! I thought we'd been overheard by some lurking scout!" declared the last speaker, and both men laughed in relief to find that it was only a girl and her doll, no doubt playing house, they thought.

"Where is General Hooker?" demanded Kathleen, and at her serious voice both men laughed again.

"It's said he crossed the Potomac on Thursday the twenty-fifth," said one of the men. "Today is Saturday the twenty-seventh and he must be near Harper's Ferry."

"Harper's Ferry," repeated the little girl gravely. At this both men laughed again, and one said, "Maybe you'd like to carry a message to the Union Army to hurry up a bit? I reckon you wouldn't have to go as far as Harper's Ferry. But I must be off. You are Miss Melvina's niece, the little Yankee girl?" he added, and Kathleen managed to reply, "Yes, sir!" Then the men hurried away, and in an instant Kathleen was making her way down the ladder, determined to be the messenger to warn the Union general that Lee's army was advancing into Pennsylvania.

"First I must leave the box for Janet and Beth," she thought. She pulled out the threads that fastened the pocket to Adelaide Mary's skirt and took out the small package. Then she had another idea: to leave Adelaide Mary for the twins, too. "Then Beth will know I didn't mean to be hateful," she thought, suddenly recalling Beth's surprised and unhappy expression when she had refused to let her hold the doll.

"I mustn't let anyone see me," Kathleen whispered to herself. She knew she could not possibly explain why she wanted to help the Union Army, for that would mean admitting she had aided a Confederate scout.

"I must help Ted's army some way!" she thought unhappily, feeling she must make up for her accidental disloyalty to the Union Army.

She crept alongside a stone wall that separated her aunt's field from the one in which the Ross cottage stood. It was now noon, and there was no one else around when Kathleen ran quickly to the cottage. Giving Adelaide Mary a good-bye hug, she set the doll on the front doorstep, sure that the twins would soon discover her.

"Now where will I put the package?" she thought, looking about to make sure that she was not being watched. "Maybe it will be better just to drop it in the path," she decided, and this she did. Then, with one more glance at Adelaide Mary, Kathleen fled back to the stone wall and ran along it until she was out of sight of the cottage. She crossed an open field to the highway and for a moment stood looking around, uncertain which direction to take. To the south was the town of Gettysburg, and beyond it she could see Cemetery Hill.

"I wonder which road leads to Harper's Ferry?" she said aloud, and then, believing that she would soon meet someone to tell her the way, and confident that she was headed in the right direction, Kathleen started off at a good pace.

In the meantime Aunt Melvina had comforted Beth, and convinced Janet that Kathleen would be sadly disappointed not to see them at lunch.

"And after lunch I know she wants you to help her teach Frisk," said Aunt Mel. "She will be back in a little while to make up. I am sure she will!"

Beth and Janet were glad to be comforted, and as Aunt Melvina walked them back to the house, the twins were again smiling and happy and ready to believe that Kathleen had not meant to be unkind. After all, Kathleen had been so generous to them before.

No one felt at all troubled by the fact that Kathleen had disappeared. Both Mrs. Webb and Aunt Melvina believed that Kathleen, ashamed of her rudeness to Beth, had gone to her room and would soon reappear quite ready to be friends with the twins.

Even when Dosia had rung the bell and everyone had gathered in the dining room except Kathleen, no one was anxious. There were no dangers to worry about. When Mrs. Webb ran up to Kathleen's room and still did not find her, she assumed that her daughter was too ashamed to come to the dining room, so she told the others to go ahead and eat.

"Kathleen cannot be far off," she said, entering the dining room, "and she will likely appear before luncheon is over." So they all took their seats. Aunt Mel had just wished that Ted were there with them, when Beth exclaimed: "Oh! Here he is—coming up the drive on Patch!" A moment later, Ted appeared in the doorway, wearing the blue uniform of a Union soldier. He saluted the company, and in the surprise of his unexpected appearance Kathleen was forgotten until, halfway through lunch, Ted exclaimed, "Where's Katydid? And how long will she visit this time?"

"She is to stay until July Fourth, and you'll see her, I expect, in a few moments," replied his mother.

"I hope so, for I'm a soldier now, and with the Confederates headed this way, Gettysburg is sure to see trouble. I won't be able to visit again for some time," he said. Then the conversation turned to preparations being made to defend the town, and Kathleen was again forgotten until much later in the afternoon. Ted finally had to leave without seeing her, and then it was discovered that Janet and Beth had also vanished.

"Very likely they are with Kathleen playing some game," suggested Mr. Webb, for it was time for the Webbs to head home. Although they were sorry to go without saying good-bye to Kathleen, Mr. and Mrs. Webb believed their little daughter was busy playing with the twins. They set off for home thinking of the marching armies that were advancing toward them and were more troubled by this than by any fear regarding Kathleen.

It was not until late in the afternoon that Aunt Melvina decided to go to the Ross cottage to get Kathleen, who, she believed, was there with the twins. As she approached the house, she saw Beth on the front doorstep with Adelaide Mary in her arms. Aunt Mel smiled.

"That is just what Kathleen would do: bring her doll to Beth," she thought. Then Janet came running out to meet her, exclaiming, "Oh! Miss Mel! Miss Mel! We have found the lost box! The one you meant to give us, with the two gold pieces in it." Aunt Mel was too much surprised to even wonder why Kathleen was not with the twins. Not until Janet had told of finding the little package "right in the path," and both the girls had joyfully thanked Aunt Mel, did she look about expectantly for her niece.

"Where is Kathleen?" she asked, and the twins stared at her in surprise. When Aunt Melvina repeated her question, Janet replied, "We don't know. We haven't seen her."

"But the doll? Where did Adelaide Mary come from?" she asked.

"When we got home, the doll was here sitting right against the door," Beth explained, "and we have been expecting Kathleen ever since."

"She must be at home after all," said Aunt Mel. Puzzled by the unexplained appearance of the missing box, and a little concerned that Kathleen had run off to hide during Ted's visit, Aunt Melvina said good-bye to the twins and started toward home.

Dosia said that Miss Kathy had not been seen, and a thorough search of the house, garden, and stable revealed no trace of the missing girl.

"If Frisk were missing I would think Kathleen had started for home, but he's safe in his stall. Whatever has happened to the child?" said Aunt Melvina, more frightened than she dared admit, even to herself.

CHAPTER 14

KATHLEEN RETURNS

WHEN DARKNESS FELL and Kathleen had not been found, Aunt Melvina sent a messenger to the Webb farm, hoping that Kathleen might be safe in her own home.

Mr. and Mrs. Webb could hardly believe that their daughter was lost, and Mr. Webb returned with the messenger to Aunt Melvina's, promising to send Mrs. Webb word the moment Kathleen was found.

But Sunday morning, June 28, 1863, dawned without news of the missing girl. It was on this day that Major-General George Gordon Meade received the news that he had been appointed commander of the Union Army. He was a Pennsylvanian and now was to defend his own state. Although uncertain as to the enemy's movements, Meade continued to move his army northward.

That day and the following were days of deep anxiety for the Webbs and for Aunt Melvina, for

Kathleen had not returned and there was still no trace of her. Janet and Beth guarded Adelaide Mary as carefully as if she were the most valuable possession in the world, and both the little girls went about with worried faces, wondering and fearful about their missing friend.

Dosia, however, declared there was no need to worry about Kathleen. "These are war times, Miss Mel; so it's likely that the folks where Miss Kathy is can't find a way to send her home. That's all. *She's* all right." And all Kathleen's relatives could do now was to hope and pray that Dosia was right and that Kathleen was indeed with friendly people who would take care of her. For now, on the night of June 30, Confederate troops from the west, from the north, and from the east were hurrying along the roads leading to "the hub of the wheel." And Meade's forces were also marching on toward Gettysburg. The two armies were about to meet in one of the greatest battles of history.

At five o'clock on the next morning, three miles from Gettysburg, Corporal Alpheus Hodges, a Union soldier in charge of the Union picket outpost, fired his carbine to warn that the Confederates were approaching. Thus began the terrible battle that was to rage over the countryside for three days.

From the cupola of the seminary building, where Kathleen had looked happily out over a peaceful scene, the Union Army's General Buford directed the opening battle, and the Confederates, under General Hill, were advancing along the Chambersburg turnpike. On that day the Union cause was to lose one of its finest generals, Major-General John Fulton Reynolds, a native of Pennsylvania.

This was not a time for children to play outside. Janet and Beth looked out the upstairs windows of their home to watch the long gray columns of Southern troops, and to exclaim over the marching Union soldiers in blue. Adelaide Mary, carefully held by Janet, gazed out as if seeking the missing Kathleen, and saw the Union forces give way before the matchless troops under Generals Hill and Ewell. The Confederates took the town of Gettysburg, and hundreds of Union soldiers were made prisoners. For two days the town was in the hands of the Confederates, but the people remained in their homes undisturbed and only few houses were damaged by the shot and shell that were hurled over the town.

Ted was one of the first to be taken prisoner, and as he saw his beloved Patch driven off by a dashing young Confederate soldier, it was difficult for the boy to keep back his tears and to remember that he was a Union soldier. He knew of Kathleen's disappearance, and with the entire countryside given over to battle, Ted feared that his little sister might never be heard from. Where he himself would be taken, he could not imagine. One of his guards, Ted noticed, was lame. This man, tall and thin with deep-set dark eyes, was called Rob by his companions and was evidently a person of some importance.

"Your name, young Yankee?" he demanded of Ted, and when the boy responded, "Theodore Webb, Junior," it seemed to Ted that the dark eyes rested on him with a keener interest. Then Rob asked, "Only son?" in a more gentle tone.

Ted nodded and was surprised when the man continued, "Any sisters?"

But at this question Ted's courage faltered with worry over his little sister, who, he felt sure, must be wandering among innumerable dangers. "One, Kathleen! And she is lost," he replied in so broken a voice that his captor looked at him with concern.

"Lost?" said the soldier. "That child has not been wandering about all this time? Didn't she reach home safely?" At these questions it was Ted's turn to be surprised.

"Have you seen her?" he cried. "A little girl with blue eyes and yellow hair? A little girl eleven years old and always smiling?" At Ted's description of his sister, Rob smiled as he asked, "When did you last see her?"

"I haven't seen her for weeks. But she was at Aunt Mel's on Saturday, and no one has seen her since; and with this raging battle from Cemetery Hill to Oak Ridge—" Again the boy's voice faltered. Instantly a friendly hand rested on his shoulder, and Ted looked up into the kind eyes of his guard.

"Don't be troubled about your sister. I'll do my best to get news of her and let you know. Very likely she is in some farmhouse nearby."

"Thank you," stammered Ted, wondering why this lame soldier would try to help either him or Kathleen.

That night both armies rested, and in the late evening the friendly guard again came over to Ted, bringing him food and drink, and again telling him not to worry about Kathleen.

The morning of Thursday, July 2, 1863, passed without any fighting, except for occasional shots fired along the skirmish line. But another terrible battle was about to begin. Union troops, under Major-General Daniel E. Sickles and General Humphreys, were massed along those beautiful country slopes and wooded hills, on Seminary Ridge, Round Top, and the Peach Orchard, and along the stone walls and quiet roads where only a few weeks earlier Kathleen had ridden Frisk in perfect safety. Early in the day the commanding officer, General Meade, quietly appeared at Cemetery Ridge, his long-bearded face worn and haggard after a sleepless night. Officers and men crowded around him, awaiting orders.

From early afternoon until darkness blotted out field and hill, the dreadful battle went on with terrible losses on both sides. General Meade fought alongside his men as the Confederates, led by Longstreet, crowded forward up the slopes of Round Top, only to be driven back.

On Friday morning, July 3, the conflict raged near Rocky Creek, in front of that very cliff where Kathleen had come to the aid of the scout, Rob. The hot July sun beat down upon brave men marching to their death.

The three-day battle of Gettysburg closed in front of Big Round Top. Lee was forced to retreat, and before noon on Saturday, July 4, 1863, his army began marching back down the Chambersburg and Fairfield roads. By nightfall, under cover of darkness and a heavy rain, Lee's defeated army was leaving Gettysburg. Pennsylvania was no longer in danger of capture by the Confederates.

Ted and the other well-guarded Union prisoners were forced to march along with the defeated Confederates that night. Once again the lame guard Rob found Ted. Marching beside him, Rob whispered, "Could you find your way home from here?"

"Sure!" Ted answered.

"Then good-bye, and good luck to you. My name is Robert Summers. Your small sister did me a big service at Rocky Creek. Tell her I will not forget it; and her pine-tree rug has started for Georgia."

"Pine-tree rug?" echoed Ted.

"She'll tell you about it. She's safe with her aunt. But fall out; drop by the roadside, and get home as best you may," commanded the guard, and Ted found himself suddenly pushed into the underbrush. There he lay fearful and trembling as the line of Union prisoners was hurried forward through the rainy summer night.

Ted scrambled over the rough ground until the sound of the marching troops grew faint and his fears of being recaptured vanished. In the darkness he could hear a slow-moving stream.

"This must be Marsh Creek," he whispered to himself. Too tired to take another step, the boy soldier crept close to the trunk of a fallen oak tree and, in spite of rain and all the dangers near at hand, he fell instantly asleep and did not awaken until sunrise the next morning.

Ted never liked to speak to anyone of his journey over Seminary Ridge to reach Aunt Mel's on that Sunday morning after the Battle of Gettysburg. Every hill and dale, every rock and rill marked the history of tragic deeds, and when the boy came in sight of his aunt's peaceful home, standing as quiet and secure as he remembered it, he gave a little shout of delight and raced down the road eager to forget all the horrors of war.

Kathleen, sitting on the porch with Janet and Beth and Adelaide Mary, was the first to discover that the hurrying boy in blue was her missing brother. At that very moment their father was searching among the wounded soldiers who were being cared for in every farmhouse and in field hospitals nearby.

"Well, Katydid! Your friend the Confederate scout sent me home!" declared Ted. Kathleen threw her arms about him, crying, "Ted, dear Ted," over and over, until Aunt Mel and Mrs. Webb came hurrying from the upstairs bedrooms where wounded soldiers were being cared for. The family rejoiced over Ted's safety and his escape from the Confederates.

CHAPTER 15

KATHLEEN'S FRIENDS

TED WAS EAGER to hear of Kathleen's adventures. That afternoon he stretched out on the broad sofa in Aunt Mel's cool sitting room, with Kathleen beside him in a wicker rocking chair, busily winding bandages. She told him everything, beginning with her encounter with the scout, his accident, and the help she had given him.

"Lucky for me, Katydid, that you didn't desert him. I'll wager neither of us would be here safe and sound if you had not helped him. But what did he mean about the pine-tree rug?" questioned Ted. To answer that question Kathleen had to go back to her birthday, and the amazed Ted listened to the story of the lost box intended for Janet and Beth, Kathleen's efforts to earn enough money to replace the gold pieces intended for the twins, and the gift from the Confederate scout that had enabled her to do this.

"Don't you remember when I pulled the tub of water over on me?" asked Kathleen, and Ted laughingly replied that he would never forget it.

"Well, my dress was in that tub, and I'd forgotten to take the gold pieces out of the pocket," explained Kathleen, and then she began the story of her adventures during the time she had been missing.

"Those men in Aunt Mel's barn said someone ought to let the Union generals know that Lee's army was marching this way," she began, "and I thought even a little girl could do that; and I'd just heard about a Confederate scout at Rocky Creek—"

"Our friend," interrupted Ted, and Kathleen nodded. There was a brief silence and then she went on, "Well, I thought I ought to do something just as quick as I could to make up for giving a Confederate scout all the information he needed." She looked at Ted questioningly, and this time it was Ted who nodded. Kathleen continued, "I walked and walked, but I didn't meet anyone to tell me the way to Harper's Ferry, and when I came to a lane leading to a farmhouse I went in to ask, and the woman wouldn't let me go out again. She said there were Confederate soldiers in Chambersburg and that I'd have to stay with her until my own folks came to fetch me; and then General Lee came—"

"What?" exclaimed Ted, sitting up and looking at his sister as if sure that he had not heard correctly. "Do you mean to say you were at General Robert Lee's headquarters all through the battle of Gettysburg?"

"I guess so. Anyway I saw him, and I like him, and I won't ever forget him," Kathleen replied solemnly. "And when my scout came after me"—at this statement Ted again exclaimed in surprise, and Kathleen nodded and continued, "Yes, my scout came after me yesterday morning before daylight, and he brought me all the way to Aunt Mel's front door. And I like him, and I like General Lee, and they are both my friends," Kathleen concluded bravely.

"That's quite a thing for a Yankee girl to say," declared Ted, but nevertheless he knew that the lame Confederate soldier had indeed proved himself a loyal friend to the Yankee girl and to her soldier brother.

Kathleen did not answer. She was thinking of a promise the Confederate scout had made her. He had said: "When the pine-tree rug reaches my little girl, she will write you a letter. Her name is Claudia Summers." Kathleen, in turn, had eagerly promised to answer any letter that she might receive from the little Confederate girl.

Nearly a week later, the Webb family started for their own home, leaving the battlefield of Gettysburg behind them. The armies of the opposing forces had occupied many miles of the surrounding countryside, but the ridges beyond the town had been the central location of the battles where General Lee's forces of more than 70,000 soldiers had been defeated by Meade's troops numbering about 93,000 men.

The Webbs were all eager to get home, but as they reached their farm, Ted's thoughts drifted unhappily to his lost horse, Patch. Hitty came running out to welcome them, full of excited questions. The family quickly assured her that her mother, Dosia, was safe and unharmed.

Meanwhile, Ted led Frisk to the stable. As he unsaddled the pony, a familiar whinny made him jump. "Sounded like Patch," he thought sadly. A second whinny made him turn quickly toward the stall that Patch had always occupied, and with an exclamation of delight the boy rushed to it, exclaiming, "Patch! Patch!" He pushed open the stall door and threw his arms around the neck of his gray horse, hugging Patch with delight.

"My goodness. I was afraid you were all dead!" Hitty announced as she helped carry Kathleen's trunk upstairs. "When the gray horse came racing into the yard, I said—"

"The gray horse! Oh, Hitty! *Is* Patch here?" exclaimed Kathleen, who had just placed Adelaide Mary into her special corner.

"Yes, Miss Kathy. The gray horse has been here nearly a week! How come you all, and my mother, weren't killed in all that fighting?" demanded Hitty, but Kathleen was already racing off toward the stable to rejoice with Ted over the return of Patch. Ted wondered what grim fate had befallen the young Confederate soldier who had taken his gray horse on that first day of battle, when Gettysburg was in the hands of the Confederates. Ted was too happy and grateful to be home safe—he no longer felt any anger against the Southern lad who had taken Patch.

Kathleen rejoiced to be back in her own home, and when her father and mother heard the story of their daughter's adventures, beginning on that June day when she had ridden off on Frisk with the pine-tree rug tied to her saddle, they felt that fortune had indeed watched over their children. For if Kathleen had not befriended the Confederate scout, their soldier son might at this moment be a prisoner of the defeated Confederates.

Ted was full of praise for the great generals who had led the Union forces to victory, and he proudly declared that Pennsylvania, the Keystone State, had furnished the heroes of the battle of Gettysburg.

"Listen," he demanded excitedly, "didn't General Meade command the army? And didn't General Reynolds fall in battle on the first day? And didn't General Winfield Scott Hancock direct and rally the troops, and command the line of battle on the second day? And they are all Pennsylvanians."

"And there were many more brave Pennsylvanians in battle," agreed Mr. Webb. "And their services to their state will not be forgotten." Ted realized that his father was proud indeed that his own son had been one of the defenders of Gettysburg.

Kathleen listened in silence. Thanks to the care and kindness of the Confederate officers who had been stationed at the farmhouse where she had found shelter, the little Yankee girl had been shielded from the dreadful sights of the terrible battles that had raged so near. But now remembering the imposing figure of General Robert E. Lee and his kindness to her, she exclaimed: "They weren't any braver than General Lee! And he didn't care if I was a little Yankee girl. He liked me just the same."

"There! Listen to the way she talks, Father!" said Ted accusingly. "What kind of a Yankee girl is she, to be praising Confederate generals?"

"Brave Americans, just the same, my boy," Mr. Webb reminded him, and Ted said no more. He had seen the heroic spectacle of the advancing Confederate ranks of Pickett and Pettigrew; he knew of the valor of Longstreet and Sorrel, and he had to admit to himself that his father was right. After that, whenever Kathleen spoke of General Lee as her friend, Ted made no complaint.

Although Adelaide Mary had been tenderly cared for by Janet and Beth, Kathleen decided that it was time her treasured doll had an entirely new wardrobe. Janet and Beth would be coming to the Webb farm for a visit in August, and she wanted Adelaide Mary to surprise the visitors by appearing in a new dress and hat.

"Her things shall all be white," thought Kathleen, "and her skirt shall have little ruffles all over it!" Mrs. Webb promised to allow Kathleen to select materials from a trunk in the attic, which Kathleen knew contained all sorts of treasures.

"May I have anything I want from that trunk?" she asked, and her mother smiled. "Yes, anything you want." So the next morning Kathleen climbed the attic stairs and made her way to the small black leather-covered trunk that stood near a window.

She knew that this trunk held rolls of cloth, bits of silk, and some partly worn garments, and Kathleen was sure she could find in it exactly what she wanted for her doll's dress.

CHAPTER 16

A GOLDEN GOWN

THE ATTIC WINDOW was open. Before exploring the contents of the treasured trunk, Kathleen seated herself near the window and looked out across the peaceful fields toward the ledges where she liked to play.

The July day was warm and fragrant with the midsummer sweetness of ripening grains, and Kathleen's thoughts wandered back to the May baskets for Janet and Beth that she had hidden among the ferns at the foot of the ledge. She recalled the conversation she had then overheard between two Confederate scouts. A little smile crept over Kathleen's face as she thought of her father's praise. For she had kept quiet so she could hear what the strangers said about the northward movements of the Confederate forces. The young Union soldier, Mason, who had shared their May Day supper had said Kathleen's news would be of the greatest help to the Union Army. He had hurried off, eager to carry the information to the commanding officer of the Northern Army.

"And maybe that helped, after all," Kathleen thought wistfully. For, in spite of the good fortune that had come to her and to Ted through her meeting with the Confederate scout, Kathleen could not forget that she had been the one who had thoughtlessly told the enemy where to find horses, cattle, and supplies. She found comfort in recalling Mason's praise.

"And I did see General Lee," she thought, with a little smile at the memory of the great general's kindly words to the little Yankee girl who had wandered into the very headquarters of the advancing Confederates.

Turning from the window, Kathleen lifted the lid of the trunk, and, kneeling before it, drew out the folds of paper so carefully tucked over its contents. She gave a little exclamation of delight, for the first thing she saw was a strip of silvery blue silk, and she could instantly imagine the beautiful cape it would make for Adelaide Mary. She held it up to admire the interwoven colors that gave the material its changing hues.

"That will be splendid!" she declared aloud, "and there is enough for a cape and a bonnet." She laid the silk on the floor beside her and again turned to the trunk, drawing out small neatly rolled packages of material left from her own and her mother's dresses. She selected bits of pretty muslin or bright-colored wool until she had a fine supply from which to sew her doll's new wardrobe.

Then she came to another layer of folded paper, and lifting this, Kathleen stared in amazement. For there, neatly folded, lay the most wonderful dress Kathleen had ever seen. It was the color of ripening corn, and she felt as if the trunk had suddenly been filled with sunlight. As she carefully lifted the long treasured gown, which Mrs. Webb's grandmother had brought from Italy half a century before, the dim attic room seemed to glow and shimmer from its golden beauty.

"It's brocade!" Kathleen whispered, holding up the dress. The soft folds revealed dim patterns of sprays of wheat and of a trailing vine with tiny leaves that seemed of pure gold.

"It's lovely! It's like a fairy dress," thought Kathleen, spreading out the long full skirt and admiring the short bodice and flowing sleeves. "Mother said I could have anything in the black trunk," she whispered, and wondered what Mrs. Webb would say if her small daughter suddenly appeared wearing this splendid dress.

"I'll dress up and surprise her!" she decided. As she glanced back into the trunk she gave a shout, for there lay a hat as beautiful as the dress. It was gold-colored straw, and around its high crown rested a white plume.

"Oh!" exclaimed the delighted girl, gently lifting the hat and placing it on her head. She looked around eagerly, wishing the attic had a mirror so she could see if this tall-crowned golden hat had instantly changed her into a grown-up lady. But the attic had no mirror, not even a broken one. Kathleen again turned to the trunk. "I guess this is all," she said, seeing only a folded black garment. It was a long cape of dull black satin.

"That would cover the dress all up," she thought, but at that moment Ted called out from the foot of the attic stairs: "Katydid? Katydid? Come on out to the pasture and we'll give Frisk his first lesson." In an instant Kathleen had bundled the golden dress and hat back into the trunk and was running down the stairs and off to the pasture with Ted.

Frisk was feeding quietly not far from the pasture fence and did not even lift his head when Kathleen called, "Frisk! Frisk!" But Ted's little gray horse gave his usual welcoming whinny at the first sight of his master and came trotting toward them.

"I wish Frisk would do this," said Kathleen as Patch bowed so low that his thick mane nearly touched the ground.

"He will just as soon as he knows you want him to," said Ted, giving Patch a tender young carrot as a reward for his good manners. Then, seeing that the pony had turned toward them, he called, "Come on,

THERE LAY A HAT AS BEAUTIFUL AS THE DRESS

Frisk. Here's one for you," and held out another carrot. Frisk approached slowly as if uncertain as to what might befall him. But he nibbled the carrot gratefully, and whinnied expectantly, hoping for more. Patch rested his head on Ted's shoulder as if looking on in amusement.

"Always give him a reward: carrots, an apple, sugar—whatever you find he likes best," said Ted as he began to teach Frisk to bend his head in response to the command: "Bow, Frisk. Bow!" He firmly pushed the pony's head down, and before the first lesson ended, Frisk had discovered that "Bow" meant bending his head as near the ground as possible and a prompt reward of carrots.

"It won't take long for Frisk to learn," declared Ted. "By the time the twins get here we'll have taught him a lot of tricks. I just hope that Janet won't try riding Patch again."

"She won't! I'm sure she won't," Kathleen promised, "but I do want the twins to have a good time. Can't we have a make-believe circus, Ted, while they are here?"

Ted shook his head. "No, ma'am! Those girls would break their necks. Maybe we can put on a play though," he added thoughtfully.

"What's a play?" questioned Kathleen.

"Oh, it's pretending to be other people: people in history, like Queen Elizabeth and George Washington; or else people out of books, like Don Quixote and Sancho Panza," replied Ted. His sister gazed at him admiringly, thinking that Ted knew more than any other boy in the whole state, and that the idea of a play was the finest possible way to entertain Janet and Beth.

"Yes! Let's have a play!" she agreed, her blue eyes shining with pleasure. "Let's play I'm Queen Elizabeth, and I'll dress up grand, in a crown and everything!" Remembering the golden dress (just what a queen would wear, thought Kathleen), the little girl skipped about as if practicing a new dance step.

But Ted shook his head.

"No, we'll make up a play of our own," he announced.

"What about?" asked Kathleen.

"Oh, I'll think up something," Ted promised. "It will be a play where you can dress up as grandly as you want to," he added, smiling at Kathleen's happy face.

"And Janet and Beth can be in it, too?" she asked. Ted promptly agreed, and they started toward the house talking of possible characters for Ted's play.

At lunch, Mr. Webb, who had just returned from a visit to Gettysburg, gave them some news. The governor of Pennsylvania, Andrew G. Curtin, had asked the cooperation of other Union states to set apart the Gettysburg battlefield as a sacred burial ground honoring those who had gallantly fought for the Union.

"And it is likely that President Lincoln will take part in the consecration services," Mr. Webb concluded.

"Will we see him? And will General Lee come?" questioned Kathleen.

"General Lee!" repeated Ted scornfully. "You ought to know better than that, Kathleen! The war isn't over, even if the Confederates did have to retreat. Is it likely Pennsylvania would ask Lee to come back?"

"No, the war isn't over, but the Battle of Gettysburg has decided the struggle," said their father. "It was the turning point of the Civil War. Even Jefferson Davis must now realize that no state has the power to defy the nation and that our land is dedicated to human liberty. The conflict between North and South must soon end in triumph for the Union. And if President Lincoln finds it possible to come to Gettysburg, it will add the final honor to that immortal field."

"Will we see President Lincoln?" asked Kathleen, nearly breathless with excitement at such a possibility, and for the moment forgetting even the golden gown and Ted's proposed play.

"Of course we will see him!" Mr. Webb replied with a smile. "And you may be sure that if President Lincoln visits Gettysburg, it will be a visit that will be remembered for as long as the town exists."

Kathleen thought of this many times in the days that followed. As she planned for the twins' visit, and as she sat on the garden-seat happily stitching on the silver-blue cape for Adelaide Mary, even when teaching Frisk to copy all Patch's accomplishments, the little Yankee girl was eagerly hoping that President Lincoln would come to Gettysburg and that, as her father had promised, she would see him and hear him speak.

CHAPTER 17

THE PLAY

EVERY DAY KATHLEEN questioned Ted about the play.

"Can't I help make it up?" she would ask, and her brother would smile and say, "Maybe. I remember you wrote verses for the May baskets, and as soon as I really decide what the play is going to be about, I'll tell you."

But although Kathleen made many suggestions, Ted said that he didn't want a play about queens.

"You just want to dress up," he said. "But I want a real play—like Columbus discovering America, or George Washington defeating Cornwallis."

"Those are not plays, they're history!" said Kathleen. "*I* want a truly make-believe play, with a queen in a golden dress, and a gypsy, and fairies that come and dance in the moonlight, and—and—and everything!"

Ted laughed good-naturedly. "All right. Go ahead and make it up. I'll bet Janet and Beth will help you; they will want performing horses!"

Kathleen's face instantly brightened. "You'll help, whatever it is, won't you, Ted?" she asked, and Ted agreed, pleased to escape the responsibility of creating a play that would please Kathleen and satisfy his own wish to represent some great figure in America's history. Kathleen now spent all her free time in the big attic, and with the windows at each end opened wide, the attic was as pleasant a place as any eleven-year-old girl could wish for. The soft summer breezes, fragrant with the scent of flowers and ripening fruit, drifted in; and summer showers made music on the shingled roof as Kathleen wrote down her list of characters for her play and made up what each one was to say.

She had told her mother of this plan to entertain Janet and Beth, and Mrs. Webb said that nothing could be better. She delighted her daughter by reading her *A Midsummer Night's Dream,* so that Kathleen was more sure than ever that a play must have fairies and a queen.

She had pulled a rickety old table close to the western window of the attic and spread out her papers on it. With Adelaide Mary on a three-legged footstool nearby, Kathleen passed many happy hours imagining what a beautiful queen in a golden dress would do and say when she discovered that she was, after all, not a queen but a gypsy child who had been brought to the castle by fairies.

"Janet can be the gypsy, who is really the queen," decided Kathleen, "but Beth is too plump for a fairy." And for days Kathleen puzzled about how the fairies of her imagination could become real. By the first week in September, when Janet and Beth, accompanied by Aunt Melvina, arrived for their long expected visit, Kathleen had completed her play. She was eager to tell the twins about the parts they were to take.

But Janet and Beth were filled with news of President Lincoln's upcoming visit to Gettysburg, so Kathleen had no opportunity to speak of her play.

"Mr. David Wills hopes that consecration services on Cemetery Hill can take place in October or early November, and that President Lincoln can surely be present," said Aunt Melvina.

"He has chosen the right place. It was there that the Union artillery were massed, and where so many brave soldiers met their death," said Mr. Webb, "and its consecration will be an occasion of national importance."

While the grown-ups discussed the plans for the memorial services on the battlefield of Gettysburg, the three girls slipped away and ran up to the attic. Kathleen was impatient to tell Janet and Beth about her play. But first the twins greeted Adelaide Mary, admiring her new cape and bonnet of silver-blue silk. Then they wanted to hear all about Patch and Frisk, and Kathleen promised that this time the twins would surely ride on her pony. "Guess what," Kathleen said, changing the subject. "I've written a play!" The twins, it turned out, knew exactly what a "play" was, for they, too, had become acquainted with the delights of *A Midsummer Night's Dream*. "What is the name of your play?" asked Janet. Just then Hitty rang the supper bell. "The Queen's Golden Gown," said Kathleen, and the three girls started down the stairs to join the family for supper.

"It's a secret—the name, I mean," Kathleen whispered as they entered the dining room, and Janet and Beth both nodded. During the meal the three girls exchanged frequent glances of understanding, while their elders spoke of the recent victory of Union armies at Vicksburg and of their hope that the great conflict between North and South would soon end in a lasting peace.

"Tell us all about 'The Queen's Golden Gown,' " urged Janet after supper as the girls went off to Kathleen's schoolroom, where a little fire of birch logs blazed in the fireplace. The girls settled comfortably on the big hooked rug before the hearth and Kathleen told them the story of her play.

"You see," she concluded, "it's all the golden dress. Just the moment the queen takes it off, you see that she is only a gypsy, because the fairies carried the real queen, when she was a tiny baby, to the gypsy camp and carried a gypsy baby to grow up a queen."

146

"But you ought to have a truly grand gold-colored dress!" said Janet. Kathleen was tempted to tell the twins all about the wonderful brocaded gown that glimmered and shone like sunlight itself, but, as she had decided to keep this a secret until the queen appeared in it, she said nothing. "Who is to be the queen?" Janet asked, and Kathleen answered quickly, "Why, of course I'm going to be queen! I wrote the play." She was a little surprised that Janet and Beth did not immediately agree that Kathleen should have the finest part and wear the finest dress. But a little silence followed, and Kathleen at last said, "And Janet is to be the gypsy."

"Then I'll be queen in the last act!" announced Janet with such satisfaction that Kathleen began to feel uncomfortable, for the play did not end that way. She now explained, "No. It's the golden dress, don't you see, that makes the queen. As long as she wears it, she *is* the queen. So she wears it all the time."

"What becomes of the *real* queen, who has to grow up a gypsy?" questioned Beth.

"Oh! She is so good to the fairies, putting honey on tiny glass plates for them each night and making little warm shelters beside trees where they can stay when it is cold, that they make her a Fairy Queen, and she has a grand castle that she can move anywhere she wants to live by just repeating a verse," Kathleen explained. Beth asked what the verse was.

"Gypsy and fairy may go where they please;
To sea or to mountain they journey with ease.
Their castles go with them all shining and fair—
So now with my castle I'll sail through the air."

Janet and Beth both looked at Kathleen with admiration.

"That's just like verses in books!" exclaimed Beth. "What am I going to be in the play, Kathleen?" she added.

Before Kathleen could answer, there was a light tap on the door followed by Ted's voice calling, "Who wants to pop corn?" Carrying a corn-popper in one hand and a small basket filled with well-ripened ears of corn in the other, he announced that the fine bed of hot coals was exactly right to pop corn. In a few moments the tiny kernels were in the popper, snapping merrily as they blossomed into white puffs of popcorn.

Kathleen ran off to the kitchen for a big yellow bowl and butter, and the girls forgot about the play as they happily crunched the delicious treat and listened to Ted's stories of the plans that Pennsylvanians were making for the battlefield memorial.

"And President Lincoln will be sure to come," the boy said, his face brightening at the thought that he might soon see the great statesman.

"Beth and I are each going to have a new dress for that day," announced Janet. "We are going to spend our gold pieces to buy them. Miss Melvina says everyone ought to look their best in honor of President Lincoln."

"Nothing could be too good for him," said Ted gravely, "not even a dress of gold," and at this Kathleen made a quick decision: if President Lincoln really did come to Gettysburg, she would wear that beautiful golden brocade. She said nothing of this to anyone, but from that day on, whenever anyone spoke of the President's visit Kathleen would again promise herself to wear the golden brocade. In that dress she would honor Lincoln and the brave soldiers who had given their lives at Gettysburg.

Mr. and Mrs. Webb and Aunt Melvina joined the group in front of the fire and shared the popcorn. When they all said their good-nights, and Kathleen and the twins started toward their rooms, Beth found a chance to again whisper her question to Kathleen: "Who am I going to be in the play?" Kathleen could only whisper back, "I'll tell you tomorrow."

CHAPTER 18

JANET'S DECISION

As KATHLEEN REMEMBERED her promise to tell Beth of her part in "The Queen's Golden Gown," she felt a little troubled. Kathleen lay awake long after the twins were sound asleep, wondering what she should say to Beth the next morning.

"She's too big for a fairy, and Janet has to be the gypsy because her eyes and hair are dark, and of course I have to be queen. Oh, dear, I guess Beth will have to be the queen's maid. She can wear a cap and a big apron and bow before me and say, 'Your Golden Highness, the gypsy desires an audience.' " Delighted with the solution to her dilemma, Kathleen smiled happily and soon fell fast asleep.

But Beth did not seem as delighted as Kathleen expected her to be when told of her part in the play. She did not say a word, nor did she even look at Kathleen as Kathleen eagerly explained, "It's the easiest part, Beth! Truly it is. You won't have to even study a bit. All you'll have to do is to bow low, like this," and with her arms extended Kathleen made a very low bow, "and then say, 'Your Golden Highness, the gypsy desires an audience.' Anybody could do that," Kathleen concluded. She wondered why Beth's cheeks flushed so deeply, and why Janet looked at her so queerly, and why neither of them had a word to say.

"Katydid! Katydid!" Ted called. So she ran off to see what he wanted, saying, "I'll be right back, and then we'll begin fixing the throne under the oak tree, and I'll tell you about the fairies." The twins found themselves alone.

"I want to go home," said Beth, tears gathering in her blue eyes as she thought about Kathleen's careless statement that Beth's part was of so little importance that anyone could take it. "I don't want to be in her old play. All Kathleen wants is to be the whole play. I want to go home."

"So do I!" declared Janet, even more angry than her sister. "Kathleen isn't going to let the real queen be queen at all. It isn't fair, and I don't want to be in it. But how can we go home, Beth? Miss Melvina wouldn't like it."

"We could just go," whimpered Beth.

But Janet shook her head. "No. That's what Kathleen did just before the Battle of Gettysburg, and it frightened everybody. I'm going to tell Miss Melvina that we want to go home; that's the best way. You stay here until I come back." Without waiting for Beth to reply, Janet darted out of the room to look for Aunt Melvina and explain as best she could, without telling of Kathleen's part in it, that she and Beth wanted to go home at once. She heard voices on the side porch, so she turned in that direction, hoping to find Aunt Melvina. But just before reaching the open door, she heard Ted's voice: "Well, if I were Janet and Beth I wouldn't take part in your play. You want to be the whole show. A queen and a gypsy, and a maid and fairies! And you're the queen! That's a great play, that is," and Ted laughed scornfully. Janet heard Aunt Melvina ask, "Do Janet and Beth like their parts?" Kathleen responded, "I didn't ask if they liked them. I just told them what they were to be."

"I see," said Aunt Mel, and now Janet listened eagerly as Aunt Melvina said, "I rather think, Kathleen, that the twins are being more polite than you are." Janet gave a little gasp of satisfaction and moved even closer to the door. "You see, they have accepted the parts you did not want to take, while you, their hostess—" At this Janet, who could now see not only Aunt Melvina but Ted and Kathleen as well, heard Kathleen's half-smothered exclamation and saw that Kathleen was crying. Without waiting to hear another word, she ran back to the weeping Beth.

"Stop crying, Beth, and wipe your eyes. Quick! Now listen! We don't want to go home. We mustn't!

It wouldn't be polite. And Kathleen will be back here in a minute to ask you to be the queen, but—" Seeing Beth's face brighten, Janet added firmly, "You can't be. That wouldn't be polite either! We're company. Whatever we do we must act like company; and when Kathleen says that you are to be queen in the first act and I am to be queen in the second act, we'll both say no. Now remember, Beth! And we'll say we want Kathleen to be queen, because we do, really. It would be silly and mean to go home. You *know* it would, Beth," urged Janet, for Beth was still sniffling unhappily. Beth thought it over, and after a few minutes she was her usual smiling self. Yes, she agreed, they could have as much fun as a gypsy and a waiting-maid as they could in the part of queen.

But Kathleen's face wore a most serious expression as she entered the room, for it had been a morning of many troubles. Her mother had asked her what she was going to wear as queen, and on hearing of Kathleen's discovery of the golden brocade, Mrs. Webb had spoiled Kathleen's excited plans. She had forgotten that the treasured gown was in the black trunk, and said, "Why, that gown is a family treasure, Kathleen, only to be worn on really great occasions! My dear girl, I'm so sorry, but I can't possibly let you have it for your play."

"Then there can't be any play," wailed Kathleen. "I made up the play to fit the dress. I'd be so careful, Mother," but Mrs. Webb shook her head.

"I'll make you a dress of fine yellow linen. I have some in the house that shines like silk; that will have to do, dear," she said.

"Could I wear it if President Lincoln were coming here?" asked Kathleen. Mrs. Webb replied that on so great an occasion as a visit from the President she might want to wear the golden dress herself. "But I'll promise you shall wear it," she added, and Kathleen reluctantly gave up her hope of wearing the beautiful gown in the play.

Right after this Ted and Aunt Mel had accused her of selfishness in keeping the best part in her play for herself, and Kathleen now returned to her visitors wishing that she had never even thought of a play.

"A circus with Frisk and Patch for trained horses, and Ted for a clown, would be a lot more fun after all," she thought. But when she discovered that neither Janet nor Beth would accept the part of queen, and when they both insisted that they thought their own parts were just as good as hers, Kathleen's spirits brightened. She told the twins that Ted had promised to have fairies appear at the right moment in the play, and that the throne under the oak tree was nearly finished.

"We'll have the play right after supper," she announced, thinking to herself that Janet and Beth Ross were the nicest girls in the whole world. Kathleen never knew about the twins' resentment of her thoughtlessness, or even imagined, how close they had come to going home.

The day passed busily and happily. Janet learned the verses Kathleen had written for the gypsy to say, and Beth practiced the maid's bow so vigorously that twice she fell flat on her face—to the amusement of herself and Janet and Kathleen. Ted announced that he had, by good fortune, persuaded a "tribe of fairies" to be on hand, and after an early supper the girls hurried away to get ready. Mrs. Webb had invited a number of neighbors to come and see Kathleen and her friends in "The Queen's Golden Gown," and in the early dusk of the September evening a little group gathered on the porch facing the big oak tree.

There was a murmur of surprise at the wonderful scenery Ted had created. The oak-tree "throne" was brightly lighted by a number of candles in tin holders. Tiny figures made of corn floss, white cotton, and leaves floated out from each side of the throne. This "tribe" of small winged figures surely looked like delicate fairies! Ted had attached a string to each fairy and connected it to a limb of the oak tree, so that he could make the fairies appear and disappear throughout the play.

The queen's gown shimmered and glowed in the candlelight. The gypsy, in a red gown that belonged to Aunt Mel, added a graceful dance to her part, and the waiting-maid bowed so low that she fell right over. At the end of the last act, the queen stepped from the throne to take the gypsy by the hand and announced, "Here is the true queen—" And quickly lifting the golden robe from her own shoulders, she placed it on Janet and disappeared into the shadows.

Everyone agreed that the play was a great success, and the actors, guests, and hosts returned to the dining room for a cup of Hitty's fine chocolate and the frosted cakes that Mrs. Webb herself had baked for them.

The girls and Ted had a small table to themselves, and as Ted sat down beside Kathleen, he smiled widely. "You're a good soldier, after all, Katydid," he said.

"That's what the Confederate scout said," Kathleen answered, for, although weeks had passed since the battle of Gettysburg, all the events connected with it—Ted's escape, the Confederate soldier's kindness, and her own adventures—were never far from Kathleen's thoughts.

Beth chatted happily about the fairies, and Janet was pleased to have been a queen in the end. As for Kathleen, she was happy with her play, and excited to think about her mother's promise that, if President Lincoln ever visited them, Kathleen should surely wear the dress of golden brocade.

She could hear the grown-ups at the long table talking hopefully of the prospect of an early peace. They said that President Lincoln would surely be present in Gettysburg on the day of the memorial services for the soldiers who had fallen.

"The day is now set: it is to be the nineteenth of November," said one of the guests and Kathleen repeated the date aloud: "The nineteenth of November!"

"What's that?" questioned Ted.

"It's the day President Lincoln is coming to Gettysburg," Kathleen replied.

CHAPTER 19

PRESIDENT LINCOLN

THE DAYS OF THE twins' visit passed quickly. They rode Frisk and Patch, they shared in the lessons in Kathleen's schoolroom, and they helped her work on the hooked rug that she had begun. It was to be exactly like the one she had given to the Confederate scout. Every day the girls talked about the play and repeated the lines Kathleen had written, and every day Ted or his father rode to Gettysburg to get the latest news on the plans for the memorial services. Seventeen Union states were going to send their chief executives to the ceremonies, and President Abraham Lincoln and his guard of honor would be the guests of Gettysburg.

Finally the twins' delightful visit drew to a close, and Ted was to drive them home. Janet and Beth said good-bye to Kathleen, telling her they had enjoyed every minute.

"Especially 'The Queen of the Golden Gown,' " added Beth, smiling. That very morning she had confided to Janet that she was glad they had not gone home the day after their arrival at Webb farm, when Beth had been so angry.

"There truly is a golden dress, Beth," Kathleen said, "and someday you will see it!"

"When will I see it?" questioned Beth, now quite sure that Kathleen and Ted could accomplish whatever they wanted to do. She imagined a gown of golden metal.

"You'll see it when President Lincoln comes!" declared Kathleen, and Beth and Janet agreed that everyone would put on their finest clothes for that occasion.

"We are to have new dresses, too," Janet reminded Beth as they waved to Kathleen.

"I shall be in uniform again when the President comes," Ted proudly announced that night on his return from Gettysburg. "And Mr. Daniel Wills told me that the President is to stay at his house, and I am to be one of the guards!" Ted looked very pleased about this honor.

"Oh, Ted! Can I go with you?" pleaded Kathleen.

"Well, I should say *not*," Ted promptly responded. "Girls can't be guards. But," he quickly added, noticing Kathleen's disappointment, "you will be sure to see President Lincoln, and if he knows you were at Lee's headquarters during the battle of Gettysburg he may want a word with you." Ted grinned cheerfully, for he often teased his small sister about the fact that she had helped a Confederate scout, and that she so admired the Confederate general Lee.

Kathleen was silent. She was too busy imagining the important ceremony and President Lincoln. She felt a thrill of pleasure that her mother had promised to let her wear the golden brocade dress.

As the days of sunny October passed and November came, the time of Lincoln's visit to Gettysburg drew near. Kathleen's thoughts centered more and more on the possibility of doing some special honor to this great man, who had by his Emancipation Proclamation freed the slaves.

"Mother, Ted is to be a guard on November nineteenth. What can I be?" she questioned on the day when Lincoln was to reach Gettysburg.

"Why, my dear, a loyal little Yankee girl, such as you have always been," replied Mrs. Webb. "I know just how you feel, dear child," she added. "We all feel that we wish there was something splendid and beautiful that we could do for Lincoln, but it is our loyalty to his ideals that would please him more than anything. I am sure of that."

But this reply did not satisfy Kathleen. She had gathered a large bunch of bittersweet, with its dark stems and pretty orange berries, and now asked if she could give that to the President.

"It's something, anyway," she said, and her mother agreed that if there were an opportunity, she could give Lincoln the bittersweet. Kathleen had to be content with this promise, and with her eagerness to wear the golden dress and the plumed hat as a sign of honor.

The special train bringing the President and his retinue reached Gettysburg on the afternoon of Wednesday, November 18, 1863, and Ted, in a new uniform, was among the proud boys in blue who welcomed him. On the next morning, the whole town was buzzing with excitement. Mr. and Mrs. Webb drove in early. They were to pick up Aunt Melvina and then go to Cemetery Hill, where the ceremony was to take place. Hitty would take Kathleen in the pony cart, meeting the Webbs at the battlefield.

"The twins will probably come with us," Mrs. Webb told Kathleen as she said good-bye. Kathleen instantly fled to the attic to put on the golden gown and the plumed hat, and then decided it would be a good plan to wear the black cape also. "I can take it off if I do speak to President Lincoln," she thought as she fastened the turquoise clasp that held the cape together.

"My goodness, Miss Kathy!" exclaimed Hitty as Kathleen came down the stairs. "Where did you find that hat?"

But Hitty was too excited over the prospect of seeing the great Lincoln, the man who had freed her people from slavery, to pay much attention to what Kathleen was wearing. Hitty was dressed in her best, and eager to be on the way to Cemetery Hill. Kathleen had just picked up her bunch of bittersweet and started toward the door when a sudden exclamation from Hitty made her look toward the highway.

"Look! Look! There they come! The President and the army!" declared Hitty, rushing from the room eager to reach the road to meet the procession. Kathleen was close behind her, unfastening the black cape as she ran so that the folds of the golden dress drifted about her like sunlight. The serious face of President Lincoln brightened a little as he noticed the queer little figure in a wonderful hat and a trailing gown that gleamed and shone. Kathleen, forgetting everything except the great Lincoln, ran toward him holding up the glowing bittersweet.

The President held up his hand, and the procession, which included Generals Schenck, Stahel, Stoneman and their staffs, came to a sudden halt. The drumbeats stopped, and the tall figure leaned from the saddle to smile kindly down upon the little girl who had so fearlessly run toward him. Behind her stood Hitty, gazing at him with worshipful eyes.

And now, at the great moment of Kathleen's life, as she gazed up into the patient face of Lincoln, she could think of nothing to say as he reached down and took the bittersweet from her hand.

"Thank you," he said gently, waving also to Hitty. Then the drum resumed its beat, and the procession moved on.

Neither Kathleen nor Hitty spoke as the two turned back to the house, but when they reached the door Kathleen said, "We'll start in a minute, Hitty." She quickly removed the brocade dress and took off the hat. When she seated herself in the pony cart a few minutes later, she was wearing the blue cashmere dress and embroidered cape that Aunt Mel had made for her.

Hitty and Kathleen were late in reaching Cemetery Hill. Ted was on the watch for them and led them to where Mr. and Mrs. Webb, Aunt Melvina, and Mrs. Ross and the twins were seated. Edward Everett of Massachusetts had finished his oration, a hymn had been sung, and President Lincoln was just beginning his dedicatory address. Sitting beside her soldier father, the little Yankee girl again looked up at Lincoln and listened eagerly and earnestly to the eloquent address whose perfect simplicity even Kathleen could understand:

"Four score and seven years ago our fathers brought forth on this continent a new nation, conceived in Liberty, and dedicated to the proposition that all men are created equal.

"Now we are engaged in a great civil war, testing whether that nation, or any nation so conceived and so dedicated, can long endure. We are met on a great battlefield of that war. We have come to dedicate a portion of that field as a final resting place for those who here gave their lives that that nation might live. It is altogether fitting and proper that we should do this.

"But, in a larger sense, we cannot dedicate—we cannot consecrate—we cannot hallow—this ground. The brave men, living and dead, who struggled here, have consecrated it, far above our poor power to add or detract. The world will little note, nor long remember what we say here, but it can never forget what they did here. It is for us the living, rather, to be dedicated here to the unfinished work which they who fought here have thus far so nobly advanced. It is rather for us to be here dedicated to the great task remaining before us—that from these honored dead we take increased devotion to that cause for which they gave the last full measure of devotion—that we here highly resolve that these dead shall not have died in vain—that this nation, under God, shall have a new birth of freedom—and that government of the people, by the people, for the people, shall not perish from the earth."

CHAPTER 20

THE END

As the Webbs drove home, Kathleen sat beside her mother on the back seat. "Mother, I gave President Lincoln the bittersweet. The procession came right by our house, and I ran out and gave it to him. He smiled at me, Mother, but he seemed sorry about something," said Kathleen. "And I couldn't think of anything to say to him."

Mrs. Webb smiled at Kathleen's serious face.

"I am glad you could give him the bittersweet, dear," she said gently. "And he halted the whole procession just to receive a gift from a child—that's the kind of man he is."

"And wasn't it lucky, Mother, that I had on the golden brocade?" Kathleen continued eagerly. "And I had on the plumed hat, too. You know you said I could wear it, Mother, when President Lincoln came?" and Kathleen looked a little questioningly at her mother. "The golden brocade!" exclaimed Mrs.

Webb, and Kathleen wondered if her mother had forgotten the promise.

"Oh, my dear girl! I meant if he ever came to our house—" but before Mrs. Webb could say more Kathleen interrupted, "But he came right past our gate! And you said yourself, Mother, that nothing could be too fine to do him honor, and you said the golden brocade was a treasure, and—"

But Mrs. Webb stopped her, saying: "I believe I am as pleased that you wore the brocade as you are, Kathleen! For now it becomes a greater treasure than ever: your grandmother wore it when she was presented to the Queen of Italy; I wore it at a great ball in Philadelphia; but now its greatest value will be that it was worn by a little Yankee girl when the great Lincoln thanked her for a bunch of bittersweet. Yes, the golden gown shall be treasured more dearly than ever because you wore it today when Lincoln spoke to you."

Kathleen's face brightened happily, and she gave a little sigh of contentment as she rested her head against her mother's shoulder.

"I wish General Lee could have been here," she said. At that her father looked at her sharply.

"Kathleen," he said, "have you forgotten that you are a Yankee girl, and that General Robert Lee is the leader of the Confederate Army?"

"I guess he can't help that," responded Kathleen, "and he looked sorry, just as President Lincoln did." Kathleen wondered a little at the glance that passed between her father and mother, but nothing more was said of Lee.

Time passed and the Civil War ended in the triumph of the Union Army. One day a letter came for Kathleen signed "Claudia Summers," thanking Kathleen for the pine-tree rug that the little Yankee girl had given the Confederate scout. Mr. Webb himself told Kathleen to be sure to answer the letter and to say that the Webb family would always gratefully remember the Confederate soldier's kindness to a little Yankee girl and to her soldier brother.